JAMES EARL HARDY

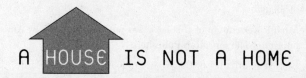

A HOUSE IS NOT A HOME

a B-Boy Blues novel

Amistad *An Imprint of* HarperCollins*Publishers*

This book is a work of fiction. The characters, incidents, and dialogue are drawn from the author's imagination and are not to be construed as real. Any resemblance to actual events or persons, living or dead, is entirely coincidental.

A hardcover edition of this book was published in 2005 by Amistad, an imprint of HarperCollins Publishers.

HarperCollins books may be purchased for educational, business, or sales promotional use. For information please write: Special Markets Department, HarperCollins Publishers, 10 East 53rd Street, New York, NY 10022.

First Amistad paperback edition published 2006.

Designed by Chris Welch

The Library of Congress has cataloged the hardcover edition as follows:

Hardy, James Earl.
A house is not a home : a B-boy blues novel / James Earl Hardy.—1st ed.
p. cm.
ISBN 0-06-621249-9
1. African American gays—Fiction.   2. African American men—Fiction.
3. New York (N.Y.)—Fiction.   4. Gay men—Fiction.   I. Title.

PS3558.A62375H68 2005   2004062774
813'.54—dc22

ISBN-13: 978-0-06-093660-0 (pbk.)
ISBN-10: 0-06-093660-6

06 07 08 09 10 BVG/RRD 10 9 8 7 6 5 4 3 2 1

To all the Pooquies & Little Bits in the world

acknowledgments

Well . . . all *jood* things must come to an end.

Hard to believe, but Pooquie, Little Bit, L'il Brotha Man, and all the other characters have been a part of my life for more than a decade. I've laughed with them, cried with them, loved with them, and most of all, learned with and from them. I never would've chosen this path to take as a writer but I am so glad it chose me. If I didn't listen to that little voice that rainy night in November 1993, I don't know where—or *who*—I'd be today. The novels have taken me places I might've never gone; introduced me to people who have become friends of the highest order; forced me to face my fears, my transgressions, my *self*; and enhanced and enriched my world in ways I am not aware of (and won't be for years to come). So, while I am sad to see this chapter come to a close, I believe that even with an ending there is a beginning. Who knows what other adventures await on the horizon. This chapter may be over, but *it* ain't over yet.

Special shout-outs to . . .

God, for the gift of life and the gift of the word. What a blessing and joy it has been to share them both.

Bam Bam: Goddaddy is so proud of the young man you've become and the man you're becoming.

Matais Pouncil, a.k.a. Mista Wonderful. *Feels like I've seen you before, maybe in a past life, you were mine and I was yours....*

Tei Black, a.k.a. Shmookie Pooh. I'll always be your one and only Baybay Boi. *What you do is crazy, baby, not like you belong in an asylum....*

Anthony Antoine, a talented musician, brutha, and friend. Your courage is very necessary in these times. Keep on keepin' it real for the Children. *Live for the dream, follow the dream, beautiful dreamer....*

The fans. I'll always cherish your testimonials and affirmations, and appreciate your patience (it is indeed a virtue!).

Luther Vandross who, for nearly a quarter-century, has inspired my work (can't ya tell?). I look forward to hearing you in concert again, soon. *Heaven knows I love you....*

And Pooquie, Little Bit, and Li'l Brotha Man, for inviting me to take this trip with them. It's been so much fun, a better-than-jood time. This might be our last dance, but it won't be the last song we enjoy together.

friday,
june 6, 2003

The routine is so familiar that Mitchell doesn't have to look at the clock to know what time it is.

At 5:45 A.M., he wakes up when he hears the hall bathroom door close. The toilet flushes at 5:47. The water faucet comes on at 5:48; when it's shut off, it's 5:55. Then the door opens and Errol's footsteps travel pass Mitchell's bedroom door and upstairs to the fourth floor, where Errol hits the treadmill and works out. When he hears Errol's footsteps coming back down the stairway, it's 6:45. Mitchell rises and heads into his own bathroom to wash up as the hall bathroom door closes again. After showering, Errol heads out of the bathroom and continues heading down the hall at 6:57.

Knock, Knock.

The voice is a mumble since Errol isn't within earshot, but Mitchell knows what Errol is saying. . . .

"Destiny? Time to get up."

Errol closes his bedroom door at seven. That's when Mitchell makes sure Destiny is up.

It took her a while to get used to rising so early. When the school year began, she'd ignore the wake-up call and turn over. After being forced out of bed by Mitchell, she'd sleepwalk to the bathroom. Sometimes she'd fall asleep while sitting on the toilet, so he'd have to watch her scrub and brush up. But now she needs no prodding or pushing. Just as he opens his own bedroom door and steps outside, she's marching into the bathroom.

At 7:01, Mitchell reaches Destiny's bedroom. He eyes the clothing hung over her rocking chair. She didn't change the outfit he chose for her the night before (let the weather warm up just a little like it has over the past few days, and she wants to wear a summer dress). He makes her bed. As he reaches Errol's room, Mitchell hears Errol's current Great Day 'N' Da Mornin' song: "Give It to Me While It's Hot," by TLC. Errol chooses a new one every week. The only artist granted more than a five-day run was Aaliyah; after her death in August 2001, she reigned with "More Than a Woman" for the entire month of September.

Mitchell puts on the coffee at 7:04 and gets *The New York Times*, which is usually stuck in one of the holes of their front gate. What he fixes for breakfast depends on what day it is. Monday is bacon, scrambled eggs, and cinammon toast. Tuesday is cereal and corn muffins. Wednesday is blueberry pancakes and turkey sausage. Thursday is oatmeal and fruit salad. On this day, Friday, "anything goes." He surprises them with one of their favorite combos: buttermilk biscuits and cheese omelets.

By the time the meal is prepared, it's 7:30. Errol is pouring their chocolate milk as Destiny enters the kitchen. "Jood morning," she sings.

"Jood morning," Mitchell and Errol respond.

As she's done so many times before, she proceeds to switch the thirteen-inch color TV that sits on the island from the *Today* show to *Little Bill*. She peers at Mitchell. "May I turn the channel?"

And, as he's done so many times before, Mitchell answers: "Yes, you may."

This is the first weekend of the month, which means Destiny will be visiting her grandparents. Errol, who normally heads up to Harlem to stay with his mother and stepfather, will remain in Brooklyn; he'll be having a party Saturday night to celebrate his fifteenth birthday.

"Are you gonna save me a piece of birthday cake?" she asks.

"Of course," Errol matter-of-factly declares, pinching her right cheek as he sits next to her.

She giggles. "Thank you."

Mitchell places their plates in front of them. He and Errol turn to Destiny, who takes both of their hands. They all bow their heads.

"God is great, God is good, thank You for our food, A-men," she sings.

"Amen," Mitchell and Errol reply together.

As Destiny laughs along with Little Bill, Mitchell and Errol talk about the party.

"Did you get ahold of that other deejay?" Mitchell asks.

"Yeah. He's got another party at midnight but it's in Crown Heights, so he can do it. He'll only charge us two hundred dollars."

"Jood."

Errol glances at the list Mitchell is making. "Oh, don't forget the blue bulbs."

"I won't. Are Sidney and Monroe coming over after school to help you set up the basement?"

"Nah, we'll do it tomorrow."

Mitchell pours himself a second cup of coffee. "You all should do it before you go to Monroe's tonight."

"Why?"

"You're going to the matinee tomorrow, right?"

"Yeah."

"That means you won't be back here until three." He examines one of Errol's twists; they've grown several inches over the past year. "It'll take at least an hour for me to touch up your hair."

Destiny pats her own 'do. "Are you gonna touch up mine, too?" She also has twists, which are shoulder-length.

"No. Yours will hold up for another week."

"Okay."

Errol takes his last bite. "But there's not that much work to do. Sweep, set up the chairs, make a space for the deejay."

He sighs. "Okay. And what about your room?"

"What about it?"

"Knowing you, it's a mess."

Errol shrugs. "It might be, but it's a manageable one."

"Yeah, I know, it may look a mess but you know where everything is."

"Right."

"At least clear a path so I can see the floor. And make up your bed."

Errol nods, turning his attention to *The New York Times*. Mitchell continues going over the shopping list; he'll make his first bimonthly trek to the supermarket at 10 A.M.

At 8:05, Destiny and Errol rise from the table. Errol takes their dishes, rinses them off in the sink, then places them in the dishwasher. She puts on her backpack; he picks up his duffel bag, placing the paper under his left arm.

"You two have a jood day," Mitchell advises.

"We will," they respond together.

Destiny picks up the remote and flips from *Blues Clues* back to the *Today* show.

Mitchell smiles. "Thank you, Sugar Plum."

"You welcome."

He hands Destiny her Little Bill lunch box; today she has a chicken-salad sandwich, sour-cream-and-onion potato chips, homemade lemonade, a banana, and raisins (her favorite food).

"Thank you," she says.

"You're welcome." He pinches her nose. "I love you."

She pinches his nose. "And I love you, too, times two!" she squeals.

They hug.

He turns to Errol. He reaches up to pinch his nose when Errol draws back. Mitchell jabs him in the left arm with his clenched fist instead, handing him his lunch. (Errol has not one, not two, but three chicken-salad sandwiches.)

Errol takes it. "Yeah, I know."

"Bye, Daddy." Destiny waves, then takes Errol's right hand as they walk out the front gate.

Mitchell waves back. "Bye, Sugar Plum."

It's now 8:08. Mitchell watches them walk to the corner, cross the street, and disappear.

If anyone had told Mitchell that he'd be raising his teenage godson and his own daughter at this point in his life, he would've laughed. Not that being a parent wasn't something he didn't ponder—or have a little practice at. Errol had been a part of his world four and a half years before Destiny arrived. But there is something about holding and molding your own that's different. And this wouldn't be a sometime or half-time (or, as it was with Errol several years ago, a one-weekend-a-month) deal. He now knew what folks meant when they said being a parent is a full-time gig.

Well, it's actually an *overtime* gig.

There's always something. A PTA meeting. A class play. A class trip. Karate lessons. A science project. A bake sale. A cold. A nosebleed. A stomachache.

And all of those things happened last *month*.

It's been a challenge but one he's been up to and met. He has made his life easier by putting the family on a schedule. Running a household comes down to time: knowing how little you've got and doing the most you can with it. He learned very early that the less he's pressed, the less he's stressed. Of course, there's always going to be stress, but you can either let it drive you crazy or you can let it drive you. He's chosen the latter.

He'd be lying, though, if he said the load didn't get heavy. It's during those times—not to mention when the ordinary that is really so extraordinary happens, such as Destiny counting to ten for the first time and Errol being smitten by the puppy-love bug—that he wishes he wasn't doing it solo. He has an idea of what his mother experienced when she became a widow.

It ain't easy being a divorced father of two.

It's been four years since he and Raheim unofficially broke up. It was unofficial because neither one of them said, "It's over," or "Get out," or "I never want to see or speak to you again." None of those things had to be said. And there weren't the usual melodramatic overreactions, like placing harassing phone calls, stalking the other at home and work, or pulling a Bernadine (torching the car and clothes, and having an all-his-shit-gotsta-go one-dollar Love's Hangover sale). They didn't have to have a mediator or court step in to defuse the situation, separate their property, force the other to pay back money owed, or issue a restraining order to keep the other away. But that didn't mean their separation was any less trying or taxing.

Up until that moment, Mitchell's world had been divided into two chapters: life before Pooquie and life with Pooquie. Life without Pooquie . . . how could he have a life *without* him? Mitchell knew, though, that it could happen . . . and not just because, statistically speaking, odds were that they wouldn't last as a couple (it's hard enough for two heterosexuals to make it work, but *two* Black same-gender-loving men?). In addition to this pressure, Mitchell feared the more Raheim got drawn into the lights, camera, and action of being a model and actor, the less lights and camera there'd be on and action there'd be in their relationship. And so it came to pass: little by little, Raheim started slipping away. He went from being very attentive to very distant. He said he'd call—and he didn't. He said he'd be there, wherever there was—and he wasn't. Even when he was around, he wasn't *there*. Mitchell once saw nothing but love in his eyes; now they were vacant and cold. Raheim became a man of very few words, yet there was so much in the words he *didn't* say. Raheim was no longer the man he'd fallen in love with; he was a stranger Mitchell sometimes shared a bed with. And Mitchell was no longer the one that Raheim turned to; he was the one Raheim turned *away* from. Mitchell had been replaced: Raheim was having an "affair" and his heart now belonged to another.

Mitchell felt helpless and paralyzed, watching what they once shared die a slow and painful death, not being able to do anything to save it. He first blamed himself: Was it something he did? Said? Didn't say or do? What could he do to make things better? He didn't know the answers, and Raheim didn't have any. He had lost faith in Raheim, had lost faith in them. And if he didn't have faith, how could he continue to give his all when he wasn't getting that all in return? He wanted to stand by his man, but how could he when his man wouldn't stand by him? He could no longer invest more than he could afford to lose. It hurt like hell, but he had to force himself to let Raheim go, to let them go. He cried over Raheim, over them, enough. He was all cried out.

And it just wasn't about them. Mitchell couldn't and wouldn't allow Errol and Destiny to watch their parents go to war or turn them into weapons to fight it. Destiny was barely two when Mitchell and Raheim parted, so she wasn't aware of the emotional gymnastics being played out. Errol was a different story: He could see and sense the tension between his father and Mitchell, and Mitchell didn't want him to think that whatever they were struggling with he had to struggle with, too, that it was in any way his fault. His father might have turned his back on Mitchell, but Errol would know that Mitchell wouldn't turn his back on him. Just because they couldn't have the family they wanted didn't mean that they wouldn't be a family at all. So Mitchell continued to nurture their family—without Raheim.

Time has healed the hurt, but it hasn't erased it. It also hasn't erased the connection Mitchell still has to Raheim—and that connection isn't simply because of Errol. In spite of the betrayal, his heart still skips a beat, although not as quick. In spite of the heartache, he still has butterflies, though the number has dwindled to about half. And in spite of the anger, he still has dreams about what their family can be.

The Emotions once asked: "How can you stop loving the one you do?"

As Mitchell has learned in the hardest way, you don't.

T his morning, Raheim is attending a "surprise" party—for himself.

It will be a very informal affair. No streamers or balloons will decorate the space. There will be no dee-jay, and music won't be played, so there won't be any dancing. Bottled water, orange juice, and soft drinks will be served, as well as punch (it won't be spiked). There will be chips and dip, cookies, maybe even a bowl of fruit (they know how much he loves bananas).

And he didn't have to dress in a shirt and tie for the occasion, but he did anyway.

When he arrives, no one is looking out so that those in attendance can hide, dim the lights, jump out, and yell surprise. He just receives handshakes, hugs, and kisses. And smiles. Miles of smiles. These people. These people from all walks and ways of life, living on the pledge. They've become more than friends; family, that's the right word. He never had a brother or sister, but most fall in those categories. And although his parents are very much alive, another couple assumed the role of father and mother, raising him up when he needed assurance and bawling him out when he needed to check himself.

No one received a personal invitation, but everyone knew to

come. And no one came with boxes or bags, but they all will be giving him a gift. Not the type one gets from a department store, through a catalog, online, or even from one of those vendors hawking their wares on sidewalks throughout the city. It's something one can't buy, something priceless.

After mingling, everyone takes a seat so the fellowship can start. The leader makes a few announcements.

And then, for what he hopes will be the very last time, Raheim stands up, smiling, and announces, with more conviction and courage than he ever has before: "My name is Raheim, and I'm a compulsive gambler."

They all smile back and respond: "Hello, Raheim. Welcome."

What a welcome it was.

The first time he said it, was at the second meeting. At the first meeting, he just sat and listened. Before the meeting began, he tried to convince himself that he didn't belong, that he didn't have a problem, that these weren't his people (and that took a lot of effort, given that he already answered yes to sixteen of the twenty "Could you be a compulsive gambler?" questions). But after that first person got up and testified, he knew he was—and that wasn't something he wanted to claim. It made him sick to realize he *was* as sick as those surrounding him and that something that appeared to be nothing more than harmless fun could destroy people's lives. Some lost their homes, their cars, their businesses, even their family and friends. Two people attempted suicide. While he wasn't that far gone, he'd gone far enough.

Every face was a different one, and all the stories they told were just as different. There was Imogene, the white woman in her sixties who squandered much of her deceased husband's million-dollar fortune at the racetrack in just two months;

Clarence, the brother in his thirties who didn't think of his bet-ting on college b-ball games as a big deal—until he forged his wife's signature to take out a second mortgage on their home; Elysa, the Dominican woman in her forties whose Lotto fever became so debilitating that she would leave the house only on Wednesday and Saturday, the days of the drawings; and Kyle, the white man who'd just turned twenty—and celebrated by losing his five-figure tuition money on the slots.

But everyone had one thing in common. Ain't no doubt about it: This addiction is an equal-opportunity fuck-u-upper.

These were the only people who truly understood what he had been through, where he was, what kind of work he had to do to get his life back, and that in order to get his life back he *had* to go back to the meetings. He didn't want to—he was afraid of what he would learn about himself and what he'd have to face—but knew he had to. He felt so guilty for letting everyone down, for letting himself down. He never dreamed he would be in a situation like this.

And just *how* did he get into a situation like this?

The seeds were planted eight years before, in 1995, when he made his feature film debut in *Rebound*. Siskel and Ebert gave the movie "two thumbs up," mainly because of him (the quote, used in all the publicity: "In one of the best performances of the year, Raheim Rivers proves that even homeboys have heart. Not since Beatrice Straight in *Network* has an actor had such a big impact with such a small role.") *USA Today* declared that he was "A Face To Watch," while *People* named him one of 1995's 50 Most Beautiful People. He grabbed the Chicago Film Critics Award for best supporting actor and there was talk of an Oscar nomination after he received Screen Actors Guild and Image Award nods. While he was passed over by the Academy and he lost the SAG and the Image Award, he picked up the In-dependent Spirit Award for best debut performance. And this night was even more special because Mitchell was by his side.

He wasn't concerned about folks figuring out they were together (especially since many of those in the world of independent cinema are gay, lesbian, bisexual, or trysexual). In his speech, he acknowledged Mitchell as his best friend and the godfather to his son. Mitchell attended a few of the after parties with him, including one hosted by the producers of *Rebound*, where Raheim was the toast of the evening. It was there that Mitchell felt comfortable enough to release the tears he had been holding in during the ceremony—and Raheim felt comfortable enough to hug him (and not in a "brotherly" way). Raheim felt so damn jood—winning and having his Baby beside him to share it with. This was the kind of party he could get used to. He never wanted it to end.

But the party did end—the next day. That's when the rejections came. He'd been passed over for roles before, the most notable being the football player in *Jerry Maguire*. At that time his agent, Troy Fauntleroy, explained that Cuba apparently had that "li'l extra something" the director was looking for. What that "li'l extra something" was, no one could say. All they knew was that Cuba had "it"—and Raheim didn't. He came really close, but not close enough. He was good, but not good enough. They liked him, but they didn't love him. He found out fast that it doesn't pay to be number two.

Yup, almost doesn't count.

He almost had that role, as well as those that eventually went to Morris Chestnut (*The Best Man*), Taye Diggs (*How Stella Got Her Groove Back*), Omar Epps (*The Wood*), Jamie Foxx (*The Players Club*), Djimon Hounsou (*Amistad*), Mekhi Phifer (*Soul Food*), Michael Jai White (*Spawn*) . . . and the list goes on. For over three years, auditioning had become his most consistent acting role. His only post-*Rebound* movie was *Dangerous Minds*, and while it was a hit, it didn't get him any additional film work (and to add insult to this injury, he wasn't approached about appearing in the TV spin-off). And if he wasn't good enough for the very few prime roles offered to Black actors each year, he knew he'd have no better luck trying out for those not written for someone Black. And he was right: Casting agents refused to see him. Nothing he did—acting classes with Howard Fine, growing a short 'fro, donning "preppy" (i.e., non-homie) attire—helped.

Now, he *did* get offers. There were those opps to play (usually) the lone Negro in horror flicks (*I Still Know What You Did Last Summer*, *Scream 2*, *Children of the Corn III*, *Leprechaun in the Hood*, and *Halloween: H$_2$O*), but he passed because spooky movies spook him out and he wasn't about to have some crazed white person chopping off his head, jamming a hook through his Adam's apple, slashing his throat, or ripping out his heart with a pitchfork—even if it was just an act. And every month he was sent at least one script in which he was asked to be The Thug. The Thug was usually identified by his criminal activity (Drug Dealer, Carjacker, Burglar, Rapist), affiliation (Gang Member, Gangbanger, Gangster), or station (Inmate). Well, he wasn't about to do a Hollywood Shuffle. While the characters he played in *Rebound* and *Dangerous Minds* were ruffnecks, they had depth, integrity, and, most importantly, *names*. They weren't nondimensional racist caricatures who are killed off thirty minutes (or in one case three minutes) after they're introduced. He wasn't about to pimp his people in the name of gettin' paid. And the only thing those roles would lead to would be more of the same. But even playing a slight variation of The Thug twice—no matter how complex or dignified those characters were—was enough to pigeonhole him.

While his movie career was a bust, he couldn't complain: After all, he continued to get featured parts on TV (*Diagnosis Murder*, *The X-Files*, *ER*, *Oz*, *Chicago Hope*, *Touched by an Angel*, *The Practice*, *Nash Bridges*, and *Homicide: Life on the Street*, which earned him an Emmy nomination for guest actor in a drama series); was still the highly paid and highly visible spokesmodel for All-American Jeans, winning male model of the year from both *GQ* and VH-1; appeared in TV commercials (from McDonald's to Toyota to 7-Up); and frequently popped up in music videos, such as Toni Braxton's "You're Makin' Me High," Lauryn Hill's "Doo Wop (That Thing)," Mary J. Blige's "Give Me You," and Will Smith's "Gettin' Jiggy wit' It." But he wanted to be known for more than his face and body, and it was his face and body that kept the dollars rolling in. Most would be content having just *one* of the options he had, but he wasn't content with any of them. After a while, being famous for your looks gets very, very old, and he became very, very frustrated. So frustrated that he caught a serious attimatude when folks asked him, "Aren't you/Ain't you/Could you be—that guy/ fella/brutha/nigga—in that ad/commercial/video/show?" After four years in the public eye, most folks still didn't know his name—and didn't seem to want to make an effort to learn it. So he'd either rebuff them ("I don't give autographs") or just lie ("Nah, I'm not him. I get that all the time"). It sounded crazy, but with everything he had goin' on, he felt like a failure. It wasn't as if he had dreams of being a movie star and he couldn't realize them. One can't have it all, and in Hollywood, one is lucky to have anything—*especially* if one is a brother. But what he had achieved, it just didn't seem . . . important. He was where he was because he just happened to be in the right place (a park), at the right time (on his lunch break), "discov-ered" by the right person (Thomas "Tommy Boy" Grayson, the VP of public relations at All-American). He was one of the lucky ones. Not talented, just lucky.

With that cloud of self-doubt hanging over his head, the devil knocked—and Raheim opened the door.

His descent into the world of gambling actually began rather innocently (as it often does for most). On one of those rare weekends when he was in New York, Mitchell suggested they get away. They hadn't been on a trip together in a couple of years (that last outing being to Disney World to celebrate Li'l Brotha Man's seventh birthday). They wanted to go to a place where they could have privacy, and they didn't want to go too far in case either one of them was called in a family emergency. So they agreed on a spa and resort in the Poconos.

They spent Saturday morning and afternoon being pampered (facials, manicures, pedicures, full-body oil massage, thermal mud baths, and all the wine, champagne, fruit, sorbet, and ice cream they desired) and pampering each other (getting lovey-dovey in the Jacuzzi). That evening, after dining at an Italian restaurant, Raheim noticed there was a casino not far from the hotel; he coaxed Mitchell into stopping in. He gave Mitchell a hundred dollars—a little "maad money" to blow. And Mitchell blew it—in fifteen minutes—on the slots. Raheim decided to try his luck at the craps table. He didn't expect to win, but did. And then he won again. And again. And again. And again. It didn't matter the combo—6 and 1, 5 and 2, 4 and 3—seven ruled, and he was the high roller makin' it happen.

Of course, a crowd gathered. The shouts and hoots grew louder. The chips got stacked higher. And the sevens kept coming.

After close to an hour, Raheim decided to cash in—and, boy, did he cash in. He turned one hundred dollars into five thousand. He and Mitchell went back to the hotel room, spilled the thousand five-dollar bills on the bed (he chose the denomination they paid him in), and they each dove into, swam in, and tossed them in the air. For Mitchell, it was jood to see Raheim relax, have fun, laugh, smile. Mitchell was happy to see him happy, and even happier to see the Pooquie he fell in love with back.

Raheim did have fun. But he didn't have fun because he was spending quality time with Mitchell, something he hadn't done in months; he had fun because of the power he felt when he rolled those dice. *This is how I would've felt if I got all those parts I came this close to getting*, he told himself. He loved this feeling and he never wanted to lose it. He finally found something that he loved to do, he could make some extra green doing, and, most importantly, he could *control* doing (or so he thought). No one would be able to dangle the joods in front of him and, when he reached for them, take them away. He'd come up with the winning number every time.

And, for awhile, he did just that during his biweekly jaunts to the Taj Mahal in Atlantic City, Foxwoods in Connecticut, or the Flamingo in Las Vegas. He had become a regular, quick; the staffs knew him and they made sure he was well taken care of—"Good evening, Mr. Rivers," "How long will you be with us this time?," "Can I get you the usual?" "If you need something, just let me know"—for they knew he would take care of them. After a month, he could walk into any of his spots and get two, five, ten Gs in credit, no questions asked. And the other gamers gave him his props; he was the *real* Goldfinger, the Man with the Midas Touch. They'd get in on his action and give him a piece of their own, buy him a drink or dinner, even offer themselves in appreciation (women *and* men).

But there was nothing like THE RUSH—the tingly sensation in his hands, the itch under his fingernails, his toes curling, the goose bumps all over his body, his heart doin' a three-step. *This is what it must feel like bein' high*, he thought. Not pissy drunk, stoned, or coked up, but *high*. Light on your feet. Dizzy. Feelin' like you can fly. Hell, it was even jooder than gettin' his bootay banged by Mitchell—and that was *really* sayin' sumthin'. Pretty soon, it replaced sex as the fix he had to have every six days.

And because he had no interest in being banged (or doin' the bangin'), Mitchell figured that he had strayed. Mitchell confronted him about being so distant, about the trips he was taking, the new clothes (such as a tacky bloodred leather suit), the flashy jewelry (a rope chain with RAHEIM spelled in diamonds), the new car (a Jeep), and the new crowd he was hanging with (folks with "names" like Tricky Ricky, Ace in the Hole, and the Joker).

When he disclosed what had been occupying his time, Mitchell was shocked—and alarmed. "Pooquie, why are you doing it?"

"*Why?* 'Cause it's fun."

"I think you should stop."

"Why?"

"Because, it . . . it's changing you."

"And that's a bad thing?"

"It is when you spend all your free time doing it. And when you're late for appointments because you're hanging at the casino."

"I was only late a couple of times."

"A couple is two; you were late five or six times."

"You keepin' count?"

"Troy and Tommy Boy have been. They called me last week about it."

"So, what, you supposed to get me in line and shit?"

"They're concerned, and I am, too. Pooquie, you . . . you've got a gambling problem."

"*Say what?*" He wasn't some potbellied, cigar-smokin' bum, spending his whole paycheck on the horses at OTB.

"You have to stop."

"Why should I?"

"So, you can't stop?"

"I can stop if I want to and I ain't. So long as I'm takin' care of thangz—"

"That's just it, you haven't been."

"Meanin'?"

"*Meanin',* you haven't been spending time with me."

"So, what, you wanna go with me?"

"Why would I want to do that?"

"The last time we hit the casino you said it was one of the best times we had in years."

"That was then. And joining you at a casino does not mean you will be spending time with *me*."

"*Me, me, me.* Is that *all* you can think about?"

"That's all *you've* been thinking about."

"And you wonder how come I ain't been spendin' time with yo' ass?"

"Don't blame me for your problem."

"I ain't *got* no problem."

"The fact that you don't think you have one *is* a problem."

"Yo, *fuck* you, a'ight? I don't need this shit."

Mitchell grasped his left arm. "Pooquie, I'm trying to help you—"

Raheim shrugged his arm off. "Help me? Whatever." He headed for the front door. He opened it.

"Pooquie, please—"

Raheim stopped.

"Please . . . don't walk out. If you walk out . . ."

He turned. "What, I can't come back?"

Mitchell stared at him, his eyes welling up with tears. "I'm . . . afraid for you."

He snickered. "You ain't gotta be." He couldn't believe how Mitchell was acting. He laughed about the whole thing on the way uptown.

But he wasn't laughing the very next day when the sevens stopped and that freewheeling feeling gave way to a tightness in his chest and tension in his neck. Where he used to clock ten Gs in one night, he was now losing it—and losing only made him want to play more. He heard a voice, a voice that had always been there, egging him on, but this time it was louder, more encouraging, ringing in his ears like an echo . . . *all it'll take is one more roll, just one more, and you can get it back, get it all back, so go for it, what do you have to lose?* And he would once again lose everything.

And you'd think that knot in his stomach would have been an indication that what he was doing was literally making him sick. The higher the loss, the more intense the pain became.

They say all compulsive gamblers have that "rock-bottom" moment. His happened when he was watching (of all things) *The Flintstones.*

That night, he had blown another bundle, his biggest loss ever—twenty-five grand (he had depleted most of his savings, CDs, and mutual funds, and now was dipping into the accounts he set up for both Li'l Brotha Man and Destiny). He decided to take a break and went to his hotel room. It was a single, smoking; he no longer received nor could he afford the royal treatment, à la the Presidential Suite. He flipped on the television and fell back on the bed—drained, exhausted, frazzled, and in excruciating pain. He heard Fred coaxing Arnold the paperboy to shoot marbles for the money he owed him, double or nothing.

Raheim immediately sat up. It wasn't as if he hadn't seen the episode before. But, for the first time, he was *seeing* it.

Fred was putting his financial future and mental health on the line—and so was he.

Fred was lying to and deceiving his loved ones—and so was he.

Fred was lying to and deceiving himself—and so was he.

Fred was a desperate man in need of desperate help—and so was he.

He caught a quick glance of himself in the mirror over the dresser. Fred was a pitiful, pathetic sight . . .

. . . and so was he.

It wasn't a coincidence that on this night, in this room, and

at this moment, he was faced with this televised characteriza-
tion of himself—and the fact that it was a cartoon made it all
the more scary.

He suddenly felt . . . COLD. That's right, COLD. Not just
chilly, but FROZEN. He crept into the middle of the bed, as if
he were recoiling in horror at something threatening. He
folded into a fetal position, wrapping himself up in his arms.
He cried the rest of the night.

He stayed in that position for a whole day. He didn't sleep.
He didn't eat. He just brooded—and burned. He felt so embarrassed. So ashamed. So *stoopid*. If he thought he was a loser before, he knew he was a loser then.

He grabbed the hotel phone and dialed. To his surprise, he
knew the digits by heart.

"Hello?"

"Uh . . . um . . ."

"Raheim, what's wrong?"

"Uh . . . uh . . ."

"What's happened?"

"I . . . I . . ."

"Just tell me where you are. I'll come get you."

He came to the hotel and brought Raheim to his apartment
in Jersey City. He had Raheim get out of his clothes and
put him to bed. He proceeded to turn off the light and leave
the room.

"Pop?" Raheim sniffled.

"Yeah, son?"

"Uh . . . don't go."

His father took a seat beside the bed. Raheim took his hand.
His father watched him sleep an entire day.

When he woke up, his father was still in that chair.

His father leaned forward. "How are you?"

"I . . . don't know."

"Are you hungry?"

He shook his head no.

"Thirsty?"

He shook his head no again.

His father squeezed his hand. "Son, you don't have to be embarrassed. Or ashamed. And don't think you're stupid."

Maybe it was the way Raheim's voice had cracked over the
phone. Maybe it was Raheim's not being able to put into words
what was happening. Maybe it was that Raheim's father, in his
own way, had been there before. Maybe it was that Raheim was
his son, and he just knew he needed him. Maybe it was all of
those things.

Whatever it was, Raheim was glad his father recognized it—
and rescued him.

But then Raheim had to rescue himself. And while there was
no one way people got in this addiction, there was only one way
out of it.

He went back to Gamblers Anonymous a third time and
thought that would be enough. But it wasn't. So he went back
a fourth time. Still not enough. Number five. Six, seven,
eight . . . He didn't think he would need the Group as much as
he had, the way he had. But he wasn't just trying to kick a very
bad habit—he was trying to get his life back.

But would the life he once had *want* him back? He'd been
walking around in a fog for several years, blind to the world
that was so important to him. And when the fog lifted, that
world was no longer there—and neither were the people who
made up that world. Sure, Little Bit and Li'l Brotha Man were
still *there*—but they were no longer *Little Bit* and *Li'l Brotha
Man*. They had done a lot of growing—individually and
collectively—in the time he was missing in action. While they
were *e*volving, he was *de*volving.

Little Bit always said he wouldn't fight *over* him but he

would fight *for* him, and he did. He hounded and harassed Raheim to stop. He left Gamblers Anonymous pamphlets around the house and in Raheim's suitcase and pants pockets. Once he tried to trick Raheim into going to a meeting. He even enlisted Raheim's mother, Angel, even Babyface, B.D., and Gene to step in and attempt to talk some sense into him. Raheim didn't feel it was anybody's business what he did and it was nobody's business what was happening between them, so he told folks to mind their fuckin' business (except his mother—he might've been out of his mind but he hadn't *lost* his mind).

And then there was the time Little Bit followed him on one of his excursions, "confronting" him at the craps table. Raheim didn't notice him standing right next to him until another gamer asked if he wanted to join in. Raheim wasn't surprised to see him there.

Their eyes locked. Little Bit didn't have to say a word; he'd already said all that needed to be said. And as far as Raheim was concerned, he had heard enough. He turned his attention back to the dice and his back on Little Bit—and let Little Bit walk away.

Raheim didn't know it then, but that was the day he forfeited the right to call Mitchell Little Bit. By not heeding Little Bit's silent cry that day, Raheim pronounced that what they had was over.

Little Bit didn't bail on him; *he* bailed on Little Bit. And Little Bit didn't break up with him because of what he had become; Little Bit broke up with him because of what he had stopped *being*.

And then there was Li'l Brotha Man. When Raheim saw him for the first time in months he almost didn't recognize him. He had grown six inches in height, standing five feet five inches. He gained forty pounds, a solid one-thirty. His shoe size went from a boy's five to a man's eight; his waist, a young man's small to a man's thirty-one. His face was rounder, fuller, and his jawline more pronounced. And his voice: no longer falsetto-ish, it had a grainier timbre, as if he'd been sucking on lemons.

His Li'l Brotha Man was literally growing up. So it shouldn't have been a surprise when . . .

Dad?

Yeah, Li'l Brotha Man?

Uh, could you do something for me?

Sure. Anything.

Uh . . . Could you stop calling me Li'l Brotha Man?

Not call you . . . why?

Because . . . I'm not exactly li'l anymore.

Uh . . . yeah. You right. You not. But what do you want me to call you?

Errol.

Errol?

Yes.

Oh. Uh, any particular reason why you wanna be called Errol?

I don't know. I guess it just fits who I am right now.

Uh . . . a'ight.

Now, Raheim could understand why he wouldn't prefer Junior, another title he wanted retired; after all, Raheim was really the "Junior" in the family. But being asked not to call his heart, his soul, his baby boy Li'l Brotha Man anymore?

If there was such a thing as a broken heart, he had one—but he only had himself to blame.

It took some time for Raheim to call him Errol. It was painful. It was a reminder that he'd *really* fucked up, that he did the very thing he said, he vowed, he *promised* he'd never do to Li'l Brotha Man—abandon him like his father did. And while he was missing in action for two years, it might as well have been twenty. He missed the highlights: his tenth birthday party, the citywide spelling championships, his elementary-school graduation, his Little League play-offs. All those things helped turn Li'l Brotha Man into Errol, and he'd become that person without him. Not only did this make his heart hurt, it made the ulcer worse. Li'l Brotha Man no longer existed, and Errol didn't see his daddy as the sun that he revolved around.

Raheim became the invisible man in the very family he wanted Crystal, Li'l Brotha Man's mother, to embrace. And she *did* embrace it—but he was no longer a part of it.

So, these strangers became his new family. They were people he would've passed in the street, people he never would have been friends with. They didn't know him, they didn't live with him, they didn't love him . . . but they understood him. They understood what he had been through, where he was, what he needed to do, and where he needed to go. He counted on them. He confided in them. He cried with them, over their heartaches and his own. And he celebrated with them—the birthdays, the births, the promotions, the engagements, the weddings, the reunions.

They didn't know it, but today would be the final time he'd fellowship with them. It was his anniversary, his one-hundredth meeting. He made the change and made the changes to stay on the right path. He felt secure enough to step out on his own. That *welcome* he received was a hello the other ninety-nine times; this time, it was a good-bye.

But he was looking forward to hearing that *welcome* again—this time, from his other family.

Mitchell couldn't open the door fast enough.

He wasn't in a rush to put away the eight bags of groceries, which he left sitting in the shopping cart just outside the hall. Yet he headed straight for the kitchen.

He tossed his keys on the breakfast table. He went into the utility closet, put the stopper in the sink, turned on the hot water, and poured in a strong mix of Ajax and ammonia. When the water was at the halfway mark, he turned off the faucet. He then gently placed both the cookie jar and its top in. He'd found it on the way home, waiting to be picked up with the five black garbage bags by the curb.

In every home, it's those little touches, those little touch-ups that give it its character. He found many of these items at flea markets throughout the city, some costing only a dollar. There's the basket-weave mirror, shaped like an open book, hanging in the first-floor foyer; the three rusted sconces, mounted diagonally just outside the great room; the navy-blue secretary with hand-painted gold bumblebees, which is in the parlor; the green elephant clock (when the alarm goes off, it bellows and the tusks rise) that Destiny keeps on her desk; the black wood, handcrafted table that's in the recreation room; the giant Ori-

ental throw rug, hanging on the basement wall; and the yellow-
ish photo of Aretha and Martin Luther King Jr., which he
framed and hung in his office.

The cookie jar, though, remained an elusive item. He'd been
searching for it since he moved into the brownstone six years
ago. Can a house *really* be a home without one? It's one of those
trappings that signal you are living "the American Dream."
But it just couldn't be *any* cookie jar; it had to be *the* cookie jar.
Only problem was he didn't know what color he wanted it to be,
how small or large it should be, what kind of design it should
have, whether it had to say COOKIE JAR, COOKIES, or nothing at
all. He must have seen hundreds of them over the years, in department stores, at street fairs, at the homes of others. But none
of them spoke to him. He'd know it was *the one* when he saw
it. And he did this morning.

This cookie jar had certainly seen better days: it was chipped
in several areas, only the outline of the word *cookies* remained,
and even after a good scrubbing some of the dark spots on its
yellow-and-off-white ceramic frame wouldn't come out. But
it didn't matter. He polished it up as if it were silver and
placed it in the space he reserved for it: in the very center of the
island. He sat on one of the dark mahogany stools, gazing at it,
beaming.

But the longer he looked at it, the less triumphant he felt. He
couldn't pinpoint why, but the moment was more bitter than
sweet. He sighed, shrugged, and retrieved the groceries, occa-
sionally glancing at it as he put them away.

When he was done, the phone rang.

"Hello?"

"Hello, I'd like to speak with Mitchell Crawford, please."

"This is he."

"Mr. Crawford, this is Emmet Paisley at Palmer Publishing
Group. How are you?"

Palmer Publishing Group. That's the company that purchased *Your World* magazine, Mitchell's former employer, several years ago. *What do they want with me?* "I'm . . . fine. And you?"

"I'm quite good, now that I have you on the phone. It took me some time, but I finally tracked you down. I have your e-mail address, but felt that introducing myself and presenting a proposal to you through that channel would be impersonal."

Hmm . . . "A proposal?"

"Yes. I'm the vice president of development in the magazine division and would like to offer you a position with our company."

"Excuse me?"

"We wish to create a new lifestyle magazine for young African-American adults, and considering your education and experience, you're our first—and only—choice to be the editor-in-chief."

Did he just hear him right? "I'm sorry?"

"We'd like you to come on board as the editor-in-chief."

Yeah, he heard him right. But this *had* to be a joke. Why would they want to hire him? Although they didn't have a hand in the racist treatment he received at *Your World,* they were aware of the million-dollar settlement he received in 1996 (it enabled him to purchase and furnish the brownstone) and the various mandated affirmative-action programs implemented because of his lawsuit.

Mr. Paisley must've known that that's where he'd immediately go. "I take it by your silence that you think this is a joke, but it's not. We know you had an unfortunate experience with one of the titles we currently publish."

Unfortunate? Try *fucked up.*

"But we hope you won't hold that history against us. And it *is* history—those individuals are no longer employed with the magazine."

Those individuals—Elias Whitley, the plagiarist and Yale

dropout promoted over him, and Steven Goldberg, the editor who kept Elias on staff after his fraud was exposed—had received their walking papers less than a month after Paisley acquired *Your World*. Steven paid a high price for their charade: after being unemployed for three years, he settled for an assistant copy-editor position at a small daily newspaper in Phoenix. But Elias's questionable credentials and character didn't prevent him from landing a plum job as a shock jock at a conservative radio station in Austin, Texas.

"Palmer is very serious about working to ensure that what we create and who we employ reflect the true diversity of the world in which we live."

Mitchell couldn't argue with him there: For the past eight years, they'd been selected by *Black Enterprise* as one of the top one hundred firms (each year they'd placed in the top thirty) for Blacks to work for *and* prosper at (too many companies will hire people of color but track them into the lowest-level, lowest-paying positions with no room for advancement or growth).

But, still, why me?

Mr. Paisley was ready for that silent query as well. "We've been following your career over the last several years—your influential stint as a creative-writing teacher at Knowledge Hall, your brilliant work in the *Times*, *Esquire*, *Essence*, and *Newsweek*. You possess the kind of journalistic integrity, critical cultural eye, writing talent, and dedication to youth that we value and need."

Okay. He knows my résumé and can lay the compliments on well. "Thank you, Mr. Paisley, but—"

"Please, call me Em."

"Uh, okay. Thanks, Em, but at this point in my writing career, I'm not sure if I want to go back to the daily grind of a nine-to-five."

What he wanted to say was at this point in his *life*. He'd gotten accustomed to (and become quite fond of his freedom as) a stay-at-home (god)father.

Em was there once again to turn a negative against Palmer into a positive. "At Palmer, it could be a ten-to-six. Or an eleven-to-seven. Even a noon-to-eight. We believe in working around the life schedule of our employees. And we know giving up the freedom you enjoy now may be hard to do. But we're willing to make you an offer you can not refuse."

Oh? Mitchell couldn't wait to hear—or, rather, read—about it.

And Em couldn't wait to let him. "Is there a number I can fax the proposal over to?"

Em was on it. Mitchell gave him the number.

"Great," Em chirped. "It'll explain the position, what the magazine's mission is, the launch schedule we're on, and a little background on us. You should receive twelve pages. If you don't, do let me know."

"All right. What's the name of the magazine?"

"It doesn't have one yet. That, along with its final look, style, and point of view, is something you, uh, the editor-in-chief will decide."

The man is focused—and persistent.

"After you've had the weekend to consider the proposal, let's talk Monday morning. Or, better yet, you can come into the office and we can discuss things in person."

Mitchell wasn't about to commit to a meeting, no matter how persuasive the man was. Besides, if he really wanted to hire him, he'd have to work on *his* timetable. "I won't be able to get back to you until Monday afternoon. If I like what I see on paper, maybe we can meet on Tuesday." He might as well enjoy this; he hadn't had many enthusiastic offers lately (truth be told, he hadn't had any).

Em was agreeable. "Okay. That's fine." Then he decided to

leave no loose ends. "If you have a question or concern over the weekend, my cell and home phone numbers will be included, so don't hesitate to call. And, if—and I do hope it's a *big* if—we can not convince you to join the staff, I'm sure we could come up with an arrangement that would satisfy us all. But do know that we would very much like to have you on board."

"Thanks. I appreciate the interest and consideration."

"No, thank *you* for the interest and consideration. You should receive the fax in the next minute. I do look forward to hearing from you on Monday—if not sooner—and working with you in the very near future. Have a good weekend."

"You too."

"Good-bye."

"Good-bye."

Ten seconds later, the fax rang. All twelve pages came through. He read the proposal in ten minutes—and ten minutes and one second was all it took.

It had been a *loooong* time since Troy, Raheim's agent, had a job for him. Not a gig—which is what his "acting" in cable series like *The Justice Files, The FBI Files*, and anything else with a *files* or *justice* in its title was— but a job. He was thankful for the work: because of the reputation he earned for not being dependable, it was a miracle that even those in the criminal-reenactment genre would take a chance on him. And the pay was jood: along with his walk-ons (the *Law & Order* franchise), commercials (Verizon Wireless, American Airlines, Amtrak, Citibank, and Target), and infomercials (yup, that's him doin' the Ab Slide and the Body By Jake), he's been able to settle his debts and begin rebuilding that nest egg.

But, after almost three years of playing the Detective, the Forensic Scientist, the State Trooper, the FBI Agent, the Prosecutor, the Judge, the Witness, and the Victim's Husband/ Father/Brother/Son (each "character" having no more than eight audible lines of dialogue in any given episode), he ached for a *real* role in a TV series (he'd like to forget the guest shots on *BeastMaster, Stargate SG-1, Xena: Warrior Princess, Tarzan*, and *Andromeda*) or, better yet, a theatrical film (his only movie appearances in the last seven years include a blink-and-you'll-miss-it cameo in *Zoolander* and three STDs, aka Straight-to-DVD releases, and he had even fewer lines in those).

So, when Raheim got the call last night that they *had* to meet today, he was excited. He knew if Troy loved the part and felt it was right for him, he'd feel the same way.

They met at the Park Avalon on Eighteenth Street and Park Avenue South. After the waiter took their order, Troy reached into his briefcase and handed Raheim the screenplay. Its white cover was stained with . . . coffee? Raheim now knew how Michael Caine felt, receiving the film projects rejected by so many others.

He saw the title. "*Dodging Me*?"

"Yes."

"What's it about?"

"It's about Glenn Burke. He was an outfielder for the Dodgers in the midseventies."

He never followed baseball, but for some reason, the name sounded familiar. He'd heard Glenn mentioned before in conversation, but it wasn't in relation to the game. It finally clicked.

"He was gay . . . ?" he half asked himself.

"Yes."

Now, if he had been given this script eight years ago when he was somewhat of a hot property, he most certainly would have passed on it. He couldn't play gay and have the world wondering if he was. But today? He's a different man with a different plan playing with a different hand.

Besides, you can't be picky when you never get picked.

So . . . "That would explain the title," he observed as he flipped the script open. He was on page twenty-five when the food arrived. And as he took the last bite of his smoked salmon, he was on ninety-nine, sixteen pages to the end.

As his clean plate was taken away, he closed the screenplay. He didn't want to know how it ended—yet.

"So?" Troy asked.

"This is a *jood* role."

"I told you."

"But . . ."

"But what?"

"Why do they want me?"

"One of the producers remembers you from *Rebound*; he saw you on *Larry King Live*."

The show, which aired two weeks ago, had focused on gambling addiction; it was Larry's in-the-news nod to high-and-flighty conservative William Bennett turning out to be a holy roller of a different kind. Gladys Knight was scheduled to participate but had to cancel, so Raheim filled her spot (yup, he was the lone Negro out of five guests). He proved to be popular with Larry (he was the only one in the studio and they had great convos during the commercial breaks) and those who called in (most addressed their comments and questions to him, including one woman who, choking back tears, said she'd be sending a tape of the program to her brother, an Internet-blackjack freak). After the show, Larry gave him an open invite to come back, and one of Raheim's fellow panelists asked him to give a speech at the National Conference on Problem Gambling in Phoenix next June (he accepted). He was pleased that he could help others get the help they needed or prevent them from going down the same path. Troy saluted his humanitarian efforts but, being the jood agent he is, saw the *King* spot for what it *really* was—a high-profile appearance that would lead to something else—and (as usual) he was right.

But . . . "So, he knows my history . . . ?" Raheim inquired.

"He does."

"And he knows I've never starred in a film before?"

"He does."

"And he still wants to take a chance on me?"

"He does."

"Wow." He exhaled. After having the door locked and bolted so long, it felt so jood to have this opportunity come his way.

And Troy knew it. "You want some time to pinch yourself?"

They laughed.

"You don't have to audition or take a screen test. I sent him a copy of *A Raisin in the Sun*, and he and the other producers loved you in it."

It was his off-off-Broadway debut. During the show's two-month run last year, he stepped out of the shadows as the understudy and into the role of Walter Lee Younger for two weeks when the star was bedridden with pneumonia. And, as luck would have it, one of those performances was filmed for a PBS special on Lorraine Hansberry. Troy coaxed the documentarians into releasing some of the footage so it could be edited and used as part of Raheim's résumé. That paid off in a big way.

"Cool. When do they want an answer?"

"As soon as possible."

"Like yesterday?"

"Yup. But we're gonna take until Monday afternoon. You haven't had this type of offer before, so you deserve to enjoy this feeling."

"Thanks. I will." He grinned.

"You're so pleased you haven't asked about the salary."

"Oh. How much?"

"Three seventy-five."

Raheim was surprised it was that much; the film would be an indie from Fine Line. He hadn't seen a six-figure check in a *loooong* time. "That'll be a nice payday."

"Indeed. But the payday wasn't nice enough for many of those they approached, probably because of the kind of role it is and the risks involved in taking it."

Yeah. Like being branded with a scarlet letter for playing a homo? Like having one's so-called masculinity questioned?

Like not being considered for "manly" roles, be they in romantic comedies or action adventures, in the future?

He brushed all that off. "They shoulda took the role *because* of the risks."

"Indeed. But their loss is your gain. This is your chance to prove that you always had it—and still do."

"Prove to who?"

"To yourself." Troy raised his glass.

He followed. They clinked. They sipped their water.

Troy glared at him. "Just don't ditch me when William Morris, CAA, and ICM come calling when the movie hits big, okay?"

After all he'd put Troy through (he'd told him "fuck you" and hung up on him more than once) and all the time Troy'd spent helping to repair his reputation and his career, the brother believed in him and stuck by him, so there's no way that would happen. "You know I won't," he promised. He smiled at the script, then frowned. "But . . ."

Troy shook his head; he was used to the doubt. "Yes?"

"What if I'm no jood? I mean, I ain't never done something this heavy before."

"Are you kidding? You were *born* to play this part. As Addison advised Eve in *All About Eve*: 'You'll give the performance of your life.' "

At 4 P.M., the second-floor doorbell rang. Destiny raced to answer it. She slowly pulled back the curtain covering one of the rectangular windows that framed the door, peeking outside.

"*Gran'ma, gran'ma!*" she squealed with utter delight upon seeing her grandmother's smiling face pressed up to the window.

As soon as Mitchell unlocked the door and there was enough space, Destiny jumped into her grandmother's arms.

"Hey there, Precious! How is my Sweetie Pie doing today?"

"I'm jood. How you?"

"I'm jood*er* now that I have you in my arms."

Destiny giggled.

As always, they spent the next two minutes cooing at each other—playing with the other's hair, pinching each other's cheeks, rubbing noses, and catching up on whatever had happened in the twenty hours since they last spoke on the phone.

The way they dote on each other, the way Mitchell's mother holds her, the way Destiny hugs her by the neck . . . you'd think she was her mother.

As it turns out, she is.

Mitchell will never forget the day—May 28, 1997. His

mother and her husband, Anderson, invited him and his brother, Adam, over to their home for dinner in Longwood, a suburb just a few miles from Newark. She told them she had a "surprise." She revealed it in their living room.

Mitchell was anxious to hear the news. "So, what's the surprise?"

"Well," she began with a pause, "I'm pregnant."

Mitchell's mouth opened—but nothing came out.

Adam didn't have that problem. *"You're what?"* He couldn't believe it.

"I'm pregnant," she repeated.

"Pregnant?" Adam winced. He said it as if it was a disease.

"Yes, pregnant."

"Are . . . are you sure?"

"Yes, I'm sure. The test came out blue—twice. And Dr. Suarez confirmed it yesterday."

Adam still couldn't believe it. "You . . . you . . . you've *got* to be kidding."

"No, I'm not."

"But, Ma, you're . . . you're . . ."

"Forty-nine? Yes, Adam, I know my age. It can happen to a woman of my years. Rarely, but it happens."

"But . . . how?"

"You know how—we had that talk when you were ten." She giggled.

"You're . . . gonna . . . have . . . a . . . *baby?"* Adam said, as if to himself, still in disbelief.

"Yes. Don't sound so excited." Her eyes fell on Mitchell. "You've been quiet about the news."

After opening his mouth a couple of times and saying nothing, he finally did. *"Wow . . ."* He turned to Adam. "We're gonna have another brother. Or our first sister."

"Whatever it is, it will be the *last* sibling you two have," she promised.

Now that he could speak, Mitchell had twenty questions. "How many months are you?"

"Two."

"So it'll be a Christmas baby?"

"Yes. My due date is the twenty-fourth."

"And Dr. Suarez said you're okay?"

"Yes. But he wants to monitor me. There are risks and there could be complications. But since I don't have anything like hypertension or diabetes, they shouldn't be anything serious if they do arise."

"And how do you feel?"

"I feel fine. I was having hot flashes and a little nausea, but it's passed. At first I thought I was going through the change. But then I got that same sensation in my belly I had when I was pregnant with you two." She rubbed her stomach.

"Will you work through the whole pregnancy?"

"Probably up until the seventh month."

"Do you plan to take some time off after it's born?"

"A year." She laughed. "You should've seen the faces of the folks I work with when I told them *why* I'd be taking a leave of absence."

Mitchell included Anderson in his next query. "What are you two hoping for, a boy or a girl?"

Anderson shrugged. "Doesn't matter. So long as it's healthy."

"I hope it's a boy," admitted Adam.

Mitchell's eyes narrowed. "Why?"

"Because then *I'll* have someone to call little brother."

"But all the kids in the family have been boys. It's about time we had a girl. I've always wanted a little sister."

"Actually," she interrupted, "she—or he—will be your sibling, but not raised as one."

"Huh?" Mitchell and Adam groaned.

"I'm not young *enough* to raise another child," she declared.

"Forty-nine isn't old," Mitchell reminded her.

"You're right, it isn't. My being pregnant is proof. But it's not about my age but the stage of life we're in. We're both looking forward to retiring; me in five years, Anderson in seven. And it takes a lot of energy and patience to be a parent. When I was in my twenties and thirties it was a struggle; in my fifties and sixties, it would be an *ordeal*. I haven't been in mommy mode for a long time—and I don't want to take that trip again."

Mitchell's eyes grew wide. "You mean . . . you're gonna put the baby up for adoption?"

"In a manner of speaking, yes." She glanced at her husband.

"We'd like you to raise the baby," Anderson revealed.

Mitchell pointed to himself. *"Me?"*

"Yes. I never thought we'd have a baby, but here we are. We couldn't have our child being raised by strangers. We want to keep him—or her—in the family. And we think this is the best solution." Anderson looked at Adam. "Since you'll be a father soon, we didn't want to triple your pleasure." Adam's wife, Lynette, would be giving birth to twins in November.

"Thanks," Adam breathed, somewhat relieved.

Mitchell was overwhelmed. "Wow. I . . . I . . . I don't know what to say."

"Well, we hope you'll say yes. It's a major undertaking. And it will be a major adjustment for you."

"And *Pooquie*," Mitchell's mother added.

Anderson nodded. "Just think about it. And talk it over with him."

"Okay. I will. We will."

"But don't take too long," his mother warned. "We would like an answer before my water breaks." They all laughed.

Even though he knew his answer would be yes, Mitchell took a week to mull things over. He planned to quit his job at Knowledge Hall six months after the baby was born and stay at home until she (or he) entered the first grade (his mother and Anderson would be depositing child-support money into an account each month that would help supplement his income free-lance writing). Given how territorial Raheim could be, Mitchell was surprised but pleased that he was just as excited about the baby (in fact, Raheim painted and decorated the nursery and built the crib himself).

At the end of his mother's first trimester, they learned the baby would be a girl. No one was happier about this news than Anderson. Why? Because, as he explained to Mitchell one afternoon as they were going over some of the adoption papers, the chances were slim to none that a female would "turn out" gay living in a household with two SGL men.

Anderson then apologized. "I'm sorry for thinking this way. It's . . . it's silly."

"It is," Mitchell agreed.

"And it's stupid."

"It's that, too."

"I mean, I see how you are with Raheim's son."

"Yes, but that's *his* son. This might have been yours."

"Uh . . . yeah."

"I'm not really shocked that you feel that way. After all, you're heterosexual."

"It's still no excuse."

"No, it isn't."

"And you'd think that after so many years being your stepfather . . ."

"You'd know better? Well, you *do* know better."

Anderson shrugged. "I guess old beliefs . . . they do die hard."

"Indeed. It's very hard to totally shake them off. They become a part of you."

"Funny thing is, I didn't really consider that until someone else mentioned it."

Hmm . . . "Was this someone else Sally?"

"Uh, yeah." Sally is Anderson's first cousin. She'd kicked out her sixteen-year-old daughter, Erica, when she discovered copies of lesbian porn videos in her room, hidden in a hole cut out in the middle of her bed's box spring. Erica was taken in by her gay uncle, whom Sally hasn't spoken to in fifteen years. Sally has been giving Erica the silent treatment for eight.

"I can hear her now," Mitchell began, scrunching his face then sneering in a hoarse voice similar to hers: " 'You gonna let *him* raise your son and turn him into a *homo*?' "

Anderson chuckled. "Something like that. I tried to brush it off, but . . . it bothered me. And the fact that it bothered me *really* bothered me. I thought I was over thinking like that."

"Well, there will always be some fragments that remain. The feeling probably isn't as strong now that you know it'll be a girl, but it probably is still there. That doesn't make you a horrible person."

"But I feel like one."

"The important thing is that you recognize it and grow from it. And you've made the effort over the years. Don't you remember asking whether seeing you walk around half-naked made me this way?"

Anderson thought back. He remembered. He looked embarrassed.

"I understood where that came from; you just didn't know. And you've come a long way since then. You didn't view my being the father of your son or daughter as negative until she put that bug in your ear, and that says a lot. Did you tell Mom?"

"No. I knew she would tell me what I already knew to be true."

"Then why did you tell me?"

"I . . . I don't know. It just seemed like the right thing to do."

"See. And you thought you didn't know any better . . ."

Anderson continued to feel guilty about it but (unbeknownst to his wife and Mitchell) felt twice as guilty about passing the responsibility of raising his only child onto someone else, especially when he had the means to do it himself. And his angst was fueled by how much more desirable and sexy he found his pregnant wife to be, not to mention the excitement he felt over seeing the ultrasound, feeling the baby kick, attending the Lamaze classes, and witnessing the birth (he didn't become ill or faint in the delivery room).

But all that changed the first time Destiny (Raheim chose her name) spent the weekend with her grandparents. The romantic cloud that hung over Anderson's prebirth experience quickly disappeared, thanks to the 2 A.M. feedings; the nerve-racking, never-ending crying; and those dreaded diaper changes. And this was the easy stuff: the older they get, the more complicated and stressful the mechanics of caring for them becomes (and the worries multiply). He couldn't get used to any of this seven days a week for the next eighteen-plus years. So he, like his wife, is always glad when that first and third Friday rolls around and Destiny visits—and almost as glad when she goes back home to her daddy on Sunday. Anderson is very content with her being *Granddaddy's* little girl.

Grandma, on the other hand, treats her like a mama's girl. And while she hasn't verbalized it, even Destiny can see that the connection they share is something that could exist only between a mother and daughter. So while the plan is to tell Destiny the whole story when she turns eighteen (she knows that she was adopted and that, in the words of her uncle Gene courtesy of *Mommie Dearest,* "Adopted children are the luckiest because they were chosen"), Mitchell predicts it will happen sooner than they think (just last month, Destiny noticed how much she looked like Grandma when she was a little girl). And given how close they are, it won't be that big a shock (or, as these revelations usually do, cause turmoil and trauma). In fact, Destiny will probably start calling her "Mama"; that's the only missing ingredient in their relationship right now.

One thing's for sure, though—she *spoils* her like a grand-mother. She knows Mitchell doesn't like Destiny to eat a lot of candy, but she will always try to sneak her a treat.

Mitchell noticed the colorful wrapper she placed into Destiny's hand as she put her down. "Mom," he huffed.

"One piece of candy ain't gonna hurt her. Besides, it's sugarless."

He caved. "Okay."

Since she didn't know the difference, Destiny was more than pleased with it. "Thank you." She popped it into her mouth.

"You're more than welcome. You ready to go?"

"Uh-huh." Her little clutch bag rested on her back, having been looped under her right shoulder. She took her grand-mother's right hand.

"Okay. We better hit the road. It'll be rush hour soon."

"You mean *slow* hour, Gran'ma. The cars don't rush."

"Right. Slow hour. And we don't want to be stuck in it, do we?"

"No!" She turned to her father, wearing a rather serious look. "Daddy, don't forget."

"I won't forget," Mitchell promised.

"Forget what?" asked Grandma.

"I made Uncle Raheim a birthday card," explained Destiny. "Daddy's gonna give it to him for me."

"Ah." She studied her son. "I don't think your daddy will forget." She knew that Errol wasn't the only one looking forward to Raheim's return tomorrow evening.

Grandma leaned forward, kissing Mitchell on the lips. "See you Sunday, darling."

Destiny followed her grandmother's lead. "See you Sunday, Daddy."

Mitchell leaned down and accepted her kiss, too. "You be a jood girl."

"I will."

"Love you both," Mitchell called out as they headed out the gate.

They turned. "And we love you, too, times two!" they both sang, dissolving into giggles like the Powerpuff Girls.

Destiny hadn't been gone five minutes when Earth, Wind & Fire showed up.

Mitchell hears them come in before he sees them. Every Friday after their lab sessions at Brooklyn Tech (today they were twenty minutes early), they invade the house. They'll drop their book bags in a chair or on the floor, and march in step into the kitchen.

They met on their first day at Tech. They were the only Black males in their homeroom freshman class—and that was (and still is) the only thing they have in common . . .

While Errol is roughly six feet, Sidney is just over five feet and Monroe falls somewhere in between.

While Errol has a swimmer's build, Sidney is a teenage bodybuilding champ and Monroe is chunky.

While Errol loves baseball, Sidney's favorite pastime is (of course) weight lifting, and Monroe's, football.

While Errol is a space nut, Sidney is fascinated with forensics and Monroe is attracted to architecture.

While Errol is a hip-hop soul kinda guy, Sid is a jazz freak (his father plays drums for the likes of Cassandra Wilson and Norman Brown) and Monroe a reggae/dance-hall fan.

While Errol is personable yet unassuming, Sidney is very quiet (unless he is ribbing Monroe) and Monroe very loud.

And they come in different shades (Errol being ebony-hued, Sidney a light caramel, and Monroe a dark brown) and wear different 'dos (twists, buzz cut, and an Afro, respectively). With so much to separate them, it's no wonder they aren't always at one another's throat. But Mitchell has yet to see them in an argument in the almost three years they've known one another. Each one's distinct personality seems to provide the balance the others need.

Which is why Mitchell nicknamed them Earth (Errol), Wind (Sidney), and Fire (Monroe). Errol is the sky, Sidney is the breeze, and Monroe is the smoke and heat.

And, since he burns rubber faster than the others, Fire always reaches the refrigerator first. "Hay, Mr. C, how you lookin'?" he announced as he pulled out the two thirty-two-ounce bottles of lemon-lime Gatorade.

Mitchell was seated at the breakfast table. "I'm lookin' jood."

"Hay Mr. C," repeated Sidney.

"Hay, Unc," said Errol. He only calls Mitchell that around his friends.

"Hey. How was school?"

"Same ol', same ol'," they all chimed as Sidney took three glasses out of the dishwasher and Errol grabbed three bananas from the fruit basket on the kitchen counter. If there's *anything* they have in common, it's food: they'll eat just about everything.

"Oh, is that the article?" Monroe asked, peeking over Mitchell's shoulder as he placed the Gatorade on the table.

"Yes, it is." He, Errol, and Sidney have been Mitchell's designated focus group the past two years: when he hears about some new trend, he quizzes them. This way, he keeps his ear to the street, always finding out what's on top and what's no longer hot, and earning his keep as a contributing editor at *Teen People*. Their reward is one of the complimentary video games or CDs Mitchell receives. This time, the topic was the increasing number of males on high-school and college cheerleading squads.

"How did it come out?" piped in Sidney.

"Very jood."

"See, told ya your sources would come through," boasted Monroe.

"Man, you ain't do nothin'," Sidney reminded him. Sidney provided an important contact for the story: an interview with his cousin in Chicago, who leads his high-school squad and was the lone Black male featured.

"Yo, it's a team effort," Monroe argued.

Errol wasn't buying it. "Yeah, someone else makes the touchdown and *you* take the glory."

Each *has* had his own glory, being quoted in different articles: Errol, on getting more students of color interested in science and math; Sidney, on steroids, which he does not and has never used (a pic of him at the school gym pumping up was also featured); and Monroe, as the child of a "multicultural" couple (not surprisingly, Mitchell had to fight to keep him in it since Monroe's father is Jamaican and his mother is Filipina, and the editors only saw the concept through the very narrow prism of Black and white). Of course, Monroe was the only member of the trio to request a hundred copies of the issue he appeared in (he had to settle for ten).

"You got another assignment for us?" Monroe asked, eager and ready.

"I might, next week. If I need your expertise, I'll let you know."

"A'ight."

"The Monica CD came today. It's on the coffee table in the family room."

"Jood." Errol grinned.

"You gotta make us copies, yo," Monroe reminded him.

"I will."

"Well, before y'all disappear upstairs—" Mitchell began.

"We gonna hook it up, Mr. C," Monroe assured him (the "it" being the basement).

"Okay." He turned to Errol, who was about to say something. "And no, I didn't forget the colored bulbs."

Errol nodded. "Cool."

"Didja see the trial on CNN last night?" Monroe asked Mitchell.

"The trial" being the one for the Morehouse student accused of attacking another student with a baseball bat after he thought he was leering at him in the shower (turns out the other student was heterosexual and peeked into his stall because he thought he was his roommate). Mitchell did catch the report last night, but... "No, I didn't. Has it gone to the jury yet?"

"Any day now, they said. You still think he's gonna get off?"

"I didn't say he would get off. There's no question he assaulted him without provocation, especially since he left the bathroom to get the bat. I just don't think he'll be convicted of the added hate-crime charge. If the student he attacked was gay, maybe. But we are talking about the South. They're not as liberal as folks on the East or West Coasts when it comes to gays and lesbians."

And *Monroe* hasn't always been as liberal about gays and lesbians. He was more than shocked to learn from Errol that Mitchell was gay; he was *flabbergasted*. Weeks after the disclosure, he finally got the courage to bring it up: "How can you be gay when you have a daughter?"

Mitchell's response? "God didn't bless a heterosexual man with equipment I don't have—or that I don't use even better."

That led to an hour of myth murdering and stereotype slashing. And after that conversation, Mitchell became Monroe's pet project—anything and everything specifically or remotely dealing with homosexuals that he reads about, sees on TV, or overhears, he asks Mitchell about. So far, the topics have included "don't ask, don't tell" ("If I was in the army, I wouldn't be comfortable knowin' a gay guy is showering or sleeping next to me"), Pedro and Sean on MTV's *The Real World* ("Why do gays need to get married?"), Matthew Shepard ("If they had such a problem with him being gay, why even mess with him?"), even John Allen Muhammad and John Lee Malvo ("You think the rumor that they were . . . together is true?"), and Ernie and Bert from *Sesame Street* ("How could people think muppets could be gay?").

Last week, it was about "homo thugs" . . .

"Ain't no such thing," Mitchell informed him.

"Whatcha mean?"

"A thug is a thug. You either are one or you aren't. Straight men don't own the patent on thuggery, and gay and bisexual men who just happen to be thugs are not some special breed."

"But I read that some get hard-core so they can pass as straight."

"I'm sure some do. But some don't *get* hard-core, they just *are*. It's a natural part of their being, it's who they are, as it is with some straight brothers. You think every straight brother who is a thug is the real thing?"

"I . . . I guess."

"Guess again. Being straight is not a prerequisite for being a thug. I know so-called homo thugs who make some straight thugs look like thug*ettes*. I've known them all my life, even when I was your age, growing up in Bed-Stuy."

"So, there's always been thugs who are gay?"

"Of course. You think they just appeared yesterday or last week or last month? For as long as there have been thugs, there have been gay ones. Believe me, I know. I've dated a few."

"You mean . . ."

"As in go out to the movies, to eat, hang out with."

"Ah . . ."

Mitchell understood the curiosity: He was Monroe's first homosexual—he'd talked about them with other heteros who knew just as little as he did, but he'd never actually talked *to* one before. And after hearing about them all his life (mainly from his father, who is a stone-cold homophobe), Monroe now had the chance to learn about them from someone who would know. That he wanted to know, that this wasn't his way of being obnoxious or a smart-ass, impressed Mitchell. He felt a little uneasy being viewed and treated as a science project, a spokesperson for the so-called gay community (he's come across too many heteros who believe that if you talk to one you've talked to all), but Mitchell carefully and clearly addressed every query.

The Morehouse controversy hit much closer to home for Monroe: it's his father's alma mater, and of course he wants his son to follow in his footsteps. Monroe's initial reaction to the incident was heterosexually typical: "He tried to push up in the shower? I woulda jacked him up, too." But as the facts came out and he discussed them with Mitchell (the lightbulb moment for Monroe coming when Mitchell asked: "Would a lesbian have the right to knock you in the head with a bat because she doesn't like straight men laying eyes on her?"), he wondered out loud if he should go to Morehouse. Mitchell almost dropped the bowl of cake mix he was whipping when he confided: "I don't know if I could go to a school where a brother treats another brother like that." That he would even consider such a thing when weighing whether to attend . . . that was the ultimate proof that their talks were having an impact.

So Mitchell doesn't mind being interrogated once a week; in fact, he looks forward to it. He's come across very few hetero Black male teens like Monroe who willingly engage in discussions about sexual orientation. Having a best friend with a gay godfather has opened up a whole new world for Monroe and he's a jood example of how the best way to challenge and defeat homophobia is through forming mutually respectful relationships between heteros and homos. At first, Monroe was a naive, ignorant know-it-all; now he's "gay-friendly" and is on his way to becoming a true ally.

"I hope he gets convicted of the hate crime," Monroe offered, taking a seat. "How you just gonna swing on somebody like that? That's what they used to do to us when we was accused of lookin' at white girls."

That he would make *that* connection . . . it made Mitchell and Errol proud. Their eyes met; they smiled.

"You still undecided about Morehouse?" Mitchell asked.

"Yeah."

"What's the percentage now?"

"Uh, sixty/forty."

"Ah. It's inching back up. If you go, that doesn't mean you support what happened. And it doesn't mean I'll have to delete you."

Monroe nodded.

"In fact, the school could use more heterosexual students like you, who are willing to speak out against antigay prejudice. You could even create a gay/straight alliance—but I'm sure your father wouldn't like that."

"You know it. The rest of his hair would fall out!"

They all laughed.

"Speaking of hair: Who did yours?" Mitchell could make out the circular design of the cornrows under the mustard-yellow skullcap. Mitchell wasn't surprised when he revealed it was . . .

"Jaleesa," Monroe cheezed. He'd had his eye on her since their sophomore year.

"You finally got her attention, huh?"

"Well, you know, what can I say!" he trumped like JJ on *Good Times*. Mitchell has the first season of the series on DVD and Monroe is hooked on it (or, rather, on JJ).

"Will she be coming with you to the party tomorrow night?"

"Come on, Mr. C. I can't come to a jam like this with a female on my arm when there's gonna be so many other honeyz in da howse."

Mitchell palmed his chest. "Forgive me."

"And I gotta give her time to recover." He patted his dome. "Massagin' this head was enough to make her almost go cray-zee."

"Yeah, and that was the *only* thing she was willin' to massage!" snapped Sidney as he and Errol chuckled.

"Man, shut up!" Monroe barked.

After tossing his banana peel in the trash, Errol uncovered the leftover lasagna from last night. Mitchell knew they'd want to finish it off after school. "Thanks for taking it out."

"You're welcome."

Sidney stared at it. He looked at Mitchell.

"It has turkey sausage in it," Mitchell assured him.

"Fat-free?" he almost whispered.

"Ninety-seven percent."

"Jood," Sidney breathed. He doesn't eat red meat. Working out six days a week, he has to watch every gram of fat he puts into his body.

Monroe doesn't (or, more aptly, doesn't want to). "*Turkey* sausage?"

Mitchell rose. "You won't know the difference."

"And even if he *could* tell the difference," added Errol, "ain't no way he'd watch us eat it."

Monroe took a plate from Errol. "You know that's right." Picking up the serving spoon Errol had just rinsed off and placed in the lasagna pan, he was about to dig in.

"Yo, man, wash your hands first!" Sidney demanded, soaping up himself.

"Oops." He did so after Sidney.

Errol cut the lasagna into eight cubed portions. He helped himself to two of them. Sidney placed one on his plate.

"Man, that's all you havin'?" Monroe asked him.

"You know I can only eat small portions," Sidney reminded him.

"Like he really cares," remarked Errol as his food warmed up in the microwave. "That just means they'll be more for him."

"No question," Monroe agreed.

Mitchell walked toward the kitchen's entryway. "What time are you all leaving?" They'll be spending the night at Monroe's.

"Around seven," answered Errol.

"Okay, I'll be in my office if y'all need me."

Sidney watched Monroe place four pieces of lasagna on his plate. "Ha, Roe might. He may need you to whip up another pan."

Monroe smiled. Mitchell and Errol chuckled.

Raheim's gone from being a homeboy to a homebody.

Chances are better than jood he can be found in one of three places on any given day, the first being a soundstage. But on average he works two days out of the week. In fact, he spends more time traveling to and from his modeling or acting jobs than he does on the set.

The second is Crunch, the gym. That's where he was after his lunch with Troy. He hit the treadmill, worked on his back and chest, then chilled in the sauna for almost an hour listening to the "Missing U" cassette tape Mitchell made him eight years ago when he went to L.A. for the first time. He found it this past March, tucked in the inside pocket of the old Nike duffel bag he took on that trip. The songs—especially his favorite, the first one on side A, Gladys Knight & the Pips' "Till I See You Again"—have taken on a different meaning now.

He pumps up three days a week, just enough to maintain his six-pack and muscular frame. But on five out of every seven, he's maxin' in his father's black leather easy chair with built-in massage in front of the TV—even on a Friday night. And this Friday was no different.

He had his usual goodies: two fruit bowls, French onion Sun Chips, microwave buttered popcorn, and his father's famous lemonade. The thirty-six-inch flat-screen TV (a present from him to his father last Christmas) would be on mute this evening, though: instead of flipping from one sensational murder case to another on Court TV and newsmagazine shows like *Dateline NBC* and *48 Hours Investigates,* he planned to finish the *Dodging Me* script and plot how he'd tackle each scene.

He was settling into the chair, had the script open to page 99, and the credits for *Wheel of Fortune* ended as a promo for John Stossel's "Give Me a Break!" segment on *20/20* was beginning when his cell rang.

"Hello?"

"Rah, whazzup?" It was Angel, his homie from way back. Before Raheim could respond, Angel answered for him. " 'Nothin' much,' right?"

"As it turns out, no."

"No? What's the dealio?"

"I got offered the lead in a movie today," he stated proudly.

"You lyin', yo!"

"Nah. I'm sittin' here memorizin' my lines."

"Congrats, brutha! What's it about?"

"Glenn Burke. He was a baseball player."

"Ah. What was he, another Jackie Robinson or somethin'?"

"Uh . . . in a way."

"Cool. You deserve it, man. You done paid your dues, overtime. We gotta celebrate. And I just happen to have comps tonight for that spot I was tellin' you about the other day."

"Nah. I just wanna chill tonight."

"You just wanna chill *every* night."

"I got a jood reason. I'm gonna be carryin' a film. I gotta prepare."

"I know you don't start filmin' on Monday."

"No, but I can't take any chances. I also gotta rest up for the party tomorrow."

"All you gotta do is be there, yo."

"Dealin' with a house full of teenagers? I'm gonna need all the rest I can get."

"You *need* to get outta that house." He sounds like Raheim's father. They've both been on him about holding himself pris-oner in the apartment. "Come on. We can have a victory din-ner before. My treat."

He ate not too long ago but never turns down free food. "A'ight. Where you wanna meet?"

"You gonna drive into the city?"

"Yeah. It'll be a hassle findin' a parkin' space, but I don't wanna be bothered with public trans."

"A'ight. You can come by the job to pick me up. I'm gonna be in the office for another hour." After graduating from Baruch in 1999 with a degree in business administration, Angel won an internship at Nickelodeon that turned into a full-time gig as a production assistant. Last November, he became an assistant producer on *The Brothers Garcia*.

"I'll be there around nine."

"Jood. See ya in a bit."

"A'ight."

"One."

"One."

"**W**ell it's about time, Mommie *Queer*est!"

Gene greeted Mitchell as they embraced at the bar in Dayo's, a Caribbean/soul-food restaurant on the outskirts of the Vill that the Children have claimed as their own on Friday nights. Mitchell was meeting Gene and his other best friends, Babyface and B.D., there for dinner. Now that all their lives had become so much more busy, they always set aside one night on the weekend each month to get together.

"If *I'm* Mommie Queerest, *you're* Auntie Mame," Mitchell shot back.

"Indeed. But the Rosalind Russell version, *not* Lucille Ball. We all *hated* Lucy in that. You don't have the kiddies this eve, so why are you late?"

"Just because the kiddies are away doesn't mean there isn't work to be done around the house."

"And just because you're a housemaker with two-point-five children does not mean you become a hermit."

"Point-five?"

"Yes. Goldie."

"Of course." Gene had purchased a goldfish for Destiny for her fifth birthday.

"And how is *my* Baby?" That's how Gene refers to Destiny;

he's one of her four godfathers (Babyface, B.D., and Raheim being the others), but knows he's number one.

"She's jood. Are Babyface and B.D. here?"

He turned to the left. "Over there." They were seated at a
booth. "I had to get my drink."

"Where's the waiter?"

"We've been waiting for him to come back for ten minutes."

A buffed Latino gent sauntered by, grinning at Mitchell.
Mitchell nodded at him. "Well, food and drink aren't what's really on the menu up in here."

"It sho' nuff ain't. But our waiter is not a smart cookie: I
asked for a cranberry and orange juice and the boy brought me
a glass of orange juice and *a* glass of cranberry juice." This is
the strongest thing Gene'll drink: he gave up the hard stuff
when 2000 rolled in. "You want somethin'?"

"Yeah. I'll have the same."

"Now, don't *not* drink on my account."

"I want to keep it light tonight. I've got a busy day
tomorrow."

Gene ordered. "And how are things shaping up for Errol's
birthday bash?"

"Fine."

"As soon as the weekend's over, we have to start planning
Destiny's."

"Her birthday isn't for another six months."

"So? You, Mr. Planning Parenthood, should talk. You've got
that house running on such a tight schedule those children
probably have to make an appointment to go to the bathroom.
Besides, she is *not* having another soiree at that House of Horror." That would be Chuck E. Cheese, where last year's party
was held. Everyone had enjoyed it except Gene. He didn't feel
anything—the atmosphere, the food, the service—was jood
enough for his Baby.

"If you have your way, she'd have it at FAO Schwarz."

A devilish grin formed across Gene's face. "Hmm . . . now *that's* an idea."

Mitchell can't get over how much mellower Gene has become in his older age—and Destiny is the reason why. All the zest and zeal he possessed was tempered by his bout with cancer in late 1996. While he beat it, he was beaten down by it—the two surgeries to remove lesions and the chemotherapy left him physically ill and spiritually spent. He didn't have to, but he resigned as head of promotion at Simply Dope Records—and then resigned himself to spending his days and nights watching everything from old faves like *The Golden Girls* and *Roseanne* to newbies such as *Judge Judy* and *Cybill*.

But after he laid eyes on Destiny, the fire returned; he found a new reason to start living again. He's worse than her grandmother and Aunt Ruth in the spoiling department: So she won't have to transport clothes and toys from one place to another, Gene makes sure she has two of everything (there are some things Mitchell refused to let him double up on, such as a hot-pink Pedal Power Chevrolet Corvette and a Barbie Sport Jeep Wrangler; these items remain at Gene's, where Destiny spends the second or fourth weekend out of every month). He's made sure she'll get the best education money can buy: Starting this fall, he'll be paying her private-school tuition and has (along with her father) set up a 529 college savings program. And, while Gene's vowed to "be around when she gives *us* grandchildren," he's made sure she'll be well taken care of when he's gone: She's replaced Mitchell as the primary beneficiary of his estate, which has grown considerably in the last few years. Once Chelsea was officially christened New York's new Caucasian queer mecca (as Gene remarked about this white flight, "The Village was gettin' *way* too dark for them"), he couldn't take all the "nordic nancies and nellies" running around. So he put his three bedroom co-op on the market in

1999 and within two weeks it was purchased by (what else?) a white gay couple for $1.25 million. Because the buyers each had seven-figure incomes (one was a theater producer, the other a VP at Viacom), they paid for the apartment with cash. Gene had the cashier's check he received at the closing blown up, viewing it as "the greatest piece of artwork I've ever seen in my life." He moved into a three-bedroom co-op in Harlem Towers; Raheim's mother is his neighbor (Gene's in building 702; she's in 810). The apartment, though, is really Destiny's domain: she has possession of two of the bedrooms (one to sleep in, the other to play in), one of the full baths (which Gene had painted pink), and two of the three walk-in closets. Gene even did something Mitchell, Babyface, and B.D. thought he'd *never* do: sell his prized stuffed animal collection (when Destiny turned two, the lion, tiger, and bear weren't cute anymore, and she was afraid to step into his apartment). One of the few items he kept were the tusks from an elephant, Destiny's favorite animal.

"Why not have the party at your place?" Mitchell remarked. "Now that your zoo has officially closed, you've got lots more room for kids to run and roam around in."

Gene's eyes narrowed. "Now, you know I'll do *any*thing for *my* Baby—but I *won't* do *that*. I'd have to make every parent sign a contract stipulating that they'll pay for any damage done by their innocent little rug rats."

"Like you wouldn't want to go on *Judge Judy*?" She's replaced Roseanne as the TV "character" Gene admires most.

Gene handed Mitchell his juice. "You know I would. But taking one of *my* Baby's friends to court? I couldn't put her through that; she'd probably lose a friend, and she'd lose respect for me." Gene caressed the small locket hanging on a gold chain around his neck; it has a pic of Destiny inside (she has an identical one with his photo). As Gene paid the bartender,

Mitchell shook his head in amazement: he never thought he'd see the day when Gene would care so much about how another person viewed him. Gene can still be a firecracker, but when it comes to Destiny, he's nothing but Jell-O.

The bartender gave Gene his change; Gene left a few dollars as a tip. Then he and Mitchell made their way through the sea of brothers (not surprisingly, Gene knew many of them) to the booth.

There they found Babyface and B.D. hugged up and rubbing noses as B.D. played with Babyface's locks, which are now past his waist. You'd think they were fourteen, not forty, the way they carry on. They'll be celebrating ten years as a "married" couple this coming Valentine's Day—and there aren't many *straight* couples who can say that. And as their love has grown, so have their careers. In 1998, Babyface left the district attorney's office, sick of trying to make cases against corrupt and abusive police officers and coming up against not only the blue wall of silence but the indifference of his own colleagues. So, with two other former New York DA's, Gerardo Gomez and Dyanna Joyce, he opened a civil practice, specializing in police brutality and race/gender/sexual-orientation discrimination cases. One of their first: a suit alleging that, with the tacit support of the Board of Education, law enforcement was allowed to take Black and Latino male students out of high schools to appear in police lineups. Within a month, a settlement was reached: $7 million, to be split between twenty-nine families. Since then, they've literally given Johnnie Cochran and his New York City firm a run for their money, racking up an additional $35 million.

While his man worked that legalese, B.D. was steppin' up a storm onstage. He's had stints in *Kiss of the Spider Woman*, *Rent*, *The Lion King*, and *Fosse*, but it was his off-Broadway show, *Fagnificent*, a hilarious riff on sissydom, that put him on the Who's Who in Theater map. Featuring his multiethnic, multigender, multiracial dance troupe, Imani, the show cleaned up at the box office and during awards season (three Obies, two Outer Critics Circle and Drama Desk Awards, and, when it moved to Broadway for nine months, a Tony for special event). It also received a Gay and Lesbian Alliance Against Defamation Award for best play, headlined the National Black Arts Festival, and was broadcast on both PBS and Showtime in consecutive years during Pride Month. After a year on the road, B.D. took and settled into a position teaching modern dance twice a week at City College in Harlem. His most recent public performance was on-screen, lifting both Catherine Zeta-Jones and Renée Zellweger in *Chicago*.

They are the Black SGL community's power couple. And they've managed to juggle all of this and parenthood, too. They had no trouble adopting Korey—and it's not because Babyface is an ace attorney who had the right connections and knew how to work the system. Truth is, there weren't any concerns that the four-year-old boy would turn gay having two gay guardians.

After all, he came to them that way.

Whether he actually is remains to be seen; he's only eight. But if he isn't, it would certainly be a shock. Korey was—and, today, is even *more* of—a firecracker. He makes Christopher Lowell look like Clint Eastwood. This was why Claude, his father (and Babyface's brother), didn't want him. Babyface's family never accepted Babyface, and he is one of the "straightest" gay men one could ever meet. So Babyface could only imagine the torture Korey must have experienced. Babyface's great-aunt Geraldine said Eloise, Korey's mom, defended and protected him from a lot of the abuse (the majority of it verbal, much of it from his father). Claude's contempt for his only son, his only child, was so strong that, while his wife was in a hospital dying from ovarian cancer (which some misguided relatives felt was her "punishment" for giving birth to an "abnormal" son), Claude began the process of putting Korey up for adoption.

(Geraldine would've volunteered but she was eighty-two.) It all brought tears to Babyface's eyes—and B.D.'s. So when they attended his sister-in-law's funeral, Babyface informed Claude that they'd take Korey. (He didn't have to discuss it with B.D.; after Babyface told him about Korey, B.D. declared, "We have to go get him.") Claude didn't put up a fight; he probably figured that Babyface and B.D. couldn't do any more damage to Korey (not realizing that he himself had done too much).

And seeing the instant connection B.D. made with Korey was further evidence to Claude that he could never embrace Korey in the same way. For B.D. and Korey, it was love at first sight. Babyface and B.D. arrived in St. Croix the night before the service, and from the moment he saw B.D., Korey clung to him. B.D. probably reminded Korey of his mother: light-skinned, pretty, and very maternal (he's got a pumped-up chest, and if he could lactate, B.D. would've breast-fed him). Korey bawled when they were leaving to stay the night with Geraldine; without asking, B.D. packed him an overnight bag. That evening, he slept in B.D.'s arms. At his mother's funeral, Korey sat on B.D.'s lap, not his father's. When he kissed his mother good-bye, it was B.D. who held him over the casket, not his father. And at the burial site, Korey mourned for his mother (once again) in B.D.'s arms. Babyface and B.D. stayed an extra two days to take care of the paperwork and then brought Korey home. They had all his clothes, toys, and books shipped; the only thing Korey carried on the plane with him was a photo of himself and his mother.

While he was pleased that his life partner and nephew had bonded, Babyface was concerned about Korey's being so flamboyant at such a young age. He and B.D. butted heads over whether and how they should discourage his overtly feminine ways. Not wanting to repress his personality, Babyface agreed that they shouldn't restrict how Korey expressed himself, but

B.D. had to promise not to go overboard in his "support"—which meant no Barbie, no Easy-Bake Oven, no pom-poms, and no jump rope (having a figure like B.D. in his life who *did* play with all those toys as a child meant he'd still get that kind of influence, anyway). Even if Korey identifies more with the opposite sex and turns out to be nonheterosexual, Babyface doesn't want him to forget that he is a boy. He's still taunted and teased by others, but at least he has a family that will stick up for and stand by him instead of joining the chorus.

He's been with them for three years; he now calls Babyface "Daddy" (he started referring to B.D. as "Uncle" the night they met). He hasn't asked about or for his natural father since the adoption—and, unfortunately, the same can be said for Claude when it comes to Korey. (Only Geraldine sends him birthday cards, Christmas presents, and calls twice a month.) Claude has remarried and has two more children, one of them "a real boy" (as he snickered to Geraldine). Chances are Korey will never know his half brother and sister.

The entire family has become media darlings. Last year they made it on the cover of *U.S. News & World Report*, under the heading THE NEW AMERICAN FAMILY. Of course, there is nothing "new" about it: Black SGL people have been assuming the roles of guardian and caretaker for generations, long before Caucasian queer men decided adoption was the new "in" thing—and Babyface and B.D. made this point on *Good Morning America* and *The O'Reilly Factor*. They also made the host of the latter program visibly uncomfortable by, as he put it, "flaunting their homosexuality" (they held hands during the broadcast; B.D. let O'Reilly know that he was uncomfortable with O'Reilly flaunting his ignorance). O'Reilly certainly would have gone to a commercial break if they'd been hugged up the way they were this evening.

Gene is disturbed by their being affectionate, but for an entirely different reason: he's still the reigning King of the Love Don't Live Here Anymore Club. "Will you two cut that shit out?" he groaned.

B.D. motioned toward Gene's drink. "There must be Haterade in that glass."

Babyface chuckled. "Hey, Mitch."

"Hey, you two." Mitchell kissed and hugged them both.

"Darling, I'm used to this one being unfashionably late because he *is* late, but not you," observed B.D.

"Don't get it twisted, *sister*," Gene snarled.

Mitchell settled in his seat. "Sorry. Did you two order yet?"

Babyface lifted his very empty glass. "Nope."

Gene sucked his teeth. "That child *still* has not returned? He's supposed to be waiting on us, we're not supposed to be waiting on him."

Babyface surveyed the room. "He'll come back once he realizes we're the only ones in here who want to order food."

"Did you get the kiddies off?" B.D. asked Mitchell.

"Yes. And what about your kiddie?"

"He's with his grandmother this weekend."

"Ah. And how is your mom?" B.D.'s mother adores her son-in-law and is even crazier about Korey. She sold her home in Suffolk, Virginia, and bought another in Hillside, New Jersey, to be closer to them.

"She's fine. Just"—he glanced at Babyface—"shocked by the news."

"What news?"

B.D. snuggled closer to his man, linking his left arm through Babyface's right and peering at him.

"We're getting married," Babyface announced.

"Again?" Gene snapped.

"Yes. But this time in Toronto, where it will be official in the eyes of the law."

Gene stated the obvious. "As soon as y'all cross the border, it won't be."

Babyface inhaled. "We won't be crossing the border. We'll be staying."

Mitchell's eyes widened. "You mean . . . living there?"

They both nodded.

Gene stared at them, aghast. "You're *moving* to Canada? Nobody moves *to* Canada. Didn't y'all see *South Park: Bigger, Longer & Uncut*?"

"If they didn't before, they are now," argued Babyface.

"Do you think you can live there?" Mitchell asked.

"We don't know, but it's something we have to try. It's important our family be recognized and respected *as* a family."

"Besides," added B.D., "we'll be buying a home in Detroit. So if we get homesick, we won't be far away."

"*Detroit?*" Gene gasped.

"*Don't* say it," B.D. warned. "Actually, it'll be a suburb outside the city. Who knows, maybe we'll have Anita or Aretha as neighbors."

That piqued Mitchell's interest. "Ha, if y'all do, me and Destiny will have to move in. Uh, when is the moving date?"

"Not for another year," explained Babyface. "I'll be keeping an eye on the legal situation over there—and over here. Maybe we'll get some jood news from the Massachusetts courts, Jersey, or right here. But if the law stands up to its current challenges over the border, we'll make that move next June."

"Is that when you'll have the ceremony, too?"

"No. That'll take place on our tenth anniversary."

They swooned. They kissed.

"Oh, good grief," Gene huffed.

"I know you don't normally participate in events where *L* is the main ingredient, but I would like you to help me and Mitch plan the wedding and reception," B.D. directed toward Gene.

"I suppose I can." Gene shrugged, trying to appear nonchalant but clearly flattered by the invitation.

"Jood. We want Destiny to be our flower girl."

"Don't you think your *son* will want to perform that role?" Gene countered.

"He may want to but he won't be," informed Babyface.

"He's gonna walk me down the aisle," B.D. expressed proudly.

"*Walk?* You two will be *sashaying.*" Gene chuckled.

B.D. rolled his eyes. He turned to Mitchell. "And we'd love for you to sing again."

"I'd love to. What song?"

"Given that you're the music man, we were hoping you'd have some suggestions. Something that fits our doing it a second time."

"Okay. I'll think about it. What about your jobs?"

"I'll be taking a leave for six months to explore opening up a practice in Canada. Gay marriage notwithstanding, discrimination still exists up there."

B.D. patted his chest. "And *I'll* officially become a housewife."

Gene coughed.

B.D. gave Gene the hand. "No comment from the pe*nile* gallery, okay?"

"You're gonna stop dancing?" Mitchell inquired.

"Chile, *pleeze,* that would be like not breathing. I'll be a housewife nine months out of the year. I've already been in contact with the folks at Michigan State University. I could be running the modern-dance program next summer."

"Mmm. Sounds like you two have everything . . . planned." Mitchell sighed. "You'll be living in another *country.*"

"Yeah. But not so far that you two can't come and visit."

Gene recoiled in horror. "*Visit Canada?*"

Babyface knew what would change his tune. "I hear

the Black Canadian Mountie population has multiplied considerably."

"*Oh?* Hmm . . . I *might* be able to squeeze in a visit each year.
Or two."

"Uh-huh." B.D. snickered.

Mitchell placed his hand on top of Babyface's, which was on
top of B.D.'s. "You might not be that far away but I'll miss you
all, terribly."

"And us, you." B.D. frowned at Gene. "And you won't say it,
but we know you're gonna miss us, too."

Gene smiled. "Of course I will . . . *b-otch.*"

B.D. sprang up, hugging him. "And we'll miss you!"

Gene tried pushing him away. "Oh, *please*. You know
that I—"

"—detest cheap sentiment!" they all roared.

Mista is yet another "underground" party for the homiez who aren't hetero to get crunk. Raheim hadn't been on the club scene in a while, and as far as he could tell he hadn't missed anything. While the space was different (yet another white establishment hosting their weekly, obligatory Negro Night), the faces weren't: Several of those present were the same closeted b-ballers, NFLers, and rappers he'd been running into for years, muggin' and mackin' with the same played-out game. And they were doing their best to look an age they passed a long time ago, stylin' in skullies and sports caps, Rocawear and Sean John, and the latest designer sneakers or that old standby, Timberland boots. And, yeah, he was a part of the tribe: he had the latter on and felt rather ... juvenile. He never thought he'd see the day when he'd think this way, but he now believes there's only three rea sons for a man to wear them: If he's a hard hat, going hunting/hiking, or *portraying* someone who works construction or is an outdoorsman. And he can't believe the time, energy, and money he spent—and *wasted*—cultivating a look and formulating an image with and around those boots. Ten years ago he wore them almost every day; today, *maybe* once a month (and that's for a job). Part of it was to project to the world that he was as hard as they come, but the reality was that he wasn't. Clothes don't make the man, they only *drape* the man, and they can't help you find yourself or define yourself. And the longer he stayed, watching the overage delinquents trying to out-gangsta one another, the more impatient toward and sickened by the whole scene he became.

And Angel could tell. "Man, don't look so down. You makin' *me* depressed."

"I'm not depressed."

"You look it. This is a celebration, remember? You should be happy, grinnin' from ear to ear. Not only are you gonna be a movie star, you did your time and came through it."

"Did my time? Man, you make it sound like I just got outta jail."

"Well, in a way you did serve a sentence. Only you decided how long it had to be so you could get yourself right."

"I guess. I . . . I just feel out of place."

"*You* feel out of place? I'm the one who had to work late and couldn't change out of this uniform." He was wearing a white shirt and dark blue slacks. His powder-blue tie was in his back pocket and his shirt unbuttoned, exposing his chest hairs. "At least you look like you belong up in here."

"Looks can be deceivin'."

Angel placed his beer on the bar. "You'll never guess what I heard."

"What?"

"Ernie was killed last night."

"Who?"

"You know, Ernie Rockland. Rock."

Yeah, Raheim knew. Rock, the guy who gunned down Raheim's boyhood homie, D.C., in 1993. Raheim heard through the grapevyne that Rock had gotten out three years ago after serving just six years of a nine-year sentence for killing D.C. "For real?"

"Yup."

"Uh . . . how was he killed?"

"They say he owed some dealer money. They shot him execution style, in the back of the head, three times."

"*Damn.*"

Angel waited for more of a response; nothing. "That's all you gotta say?"

"What else is there to say?"

"I don't know. I guess I just thought you'd be . . . glad."

"Glad? Why would I be glad somebody got killed?"

"This just ain't somebody."

"I know. I wouldn't wish that shit on anybody, not even my worst enemy, and *he* was it."

"Yeah. I know it's wrong to think but . . . I'm glad he's dead."

"I understand." Raheim noticed a brutha checking out Angel. "Go on over, yo."

"Nah, nah, I ain't ditchin' my boyee."

"You won't be ditchin' me. Go on and have a jood time."

"I asked you to come out so *we* could have a jood time."

"I'll have a jood time watchin' you. I can hold it down."

Angel gave the brutha a once-over. "You sure?"

"Yeah."

"A'ight. I won't be gone long."

He walked over. They did the brutha shake and a few minutes later they were doin' the booty shake on the dance floor. A half hour had passed when they parted. Angel returned with a big grin on his face.

"You look happy," Raheim observed.

"Yeah," he cheezed.

"Where he go?"

"To the bathroom."

"Ah. What's his name?"

"Jazz."

"Jazz? Like the music?"

"Yeah. And he said his mama named him that."

"A'ight."

"The brutha is *phyne*—so long as he keeps his mouth *closed.*"

"Why?"

"He's got gold covering the top row of his teeth, and platinum on the bottom."

Raheim giggled. "You lyin'?"

"Nope. The light hit 'em and I *swear* I was blinded for a second. Ya gotta wonder how he can brush his teeth."

"Ha, or if he does." Raheim downed the last of his ginger ale and stood up. "I'm gonna head out, yo."

"Man, it's not even midnight. The party ain't even get started yet."

"You got yourself some company, so the party just started for you. It's over for me."

This time Angel caught someone peepin' Raheim. "Not if *he* has anything to say about it."

Raheim's eyes focused on who Angel was referring to—and they *bugged.* Bopping straight toward them was Malice, the rapper turned hip-hop mogul. After a couple of million-selling CDs in the mid-nineties, the hits stopped for him and began for his kids. Taking a cue from Master P, he'd been grooming his own son and daughter, who are twins, for the business since they were toddlers. Li'l Lou (Malice Jr., whose middle name is Lewis) sounds a lot like Tevin Campbell, and Melanie (her real first name) borrows from Brandy. Their self-titled debuts, as well as an EP they did together *(Best Friends)*, went double platinum. Malice wrote, produced, arranged, and released all three on his own label, No Malice, and has also served as their manager, agent, and tour coordinator. And it's truly a family affair: their mother accompanies them on the road, attending all public events as their chaperon.

Raheim told Angel about him and Malice hookin' up—but

not about his being set up by Malice to be set upon by a half dozen of his hood rat boyz in a hotel room in Los Angeles. Raheim had seen Malice only once since that night eight years ago, and that was one time too many. Next to Ernie Rockland, he was the very *last* person Raheim wanted to see.

But judging by the bear smooch Malice gave him, Raheim was *just* the man Malice wanted to see. "Yo, nigga, whazzup?"

"Whazzup," Raheim mumbled.

"Man, I was just talkin' about yo' ass."

"Uh-huh," Raheim grunted. "Malice, this is Angel. Angel, Malice."

They brutha-shook.

"Whazzup, A?"

"Yo, man, it's great to meet you. My daughter is a big fan of your son."

"Oh yeah? He'll be at the Virgin megastore in Times Square signin' and singin' from his new CD in two weeks." He went into his back pocket; he handed Angel a postcard announcing the CD's release and details on the Virgin event and others in the New York area, including appearances on BET's *106 & Park* and MTV's *TRL*. Raheim heard he never went anywhere without some kind of promotional material on his kids. "Make sure she comes out."

"Thanks. She's gonna love this." Angel spotted Jazz. "Uh, I gotta go. But you take jood care of my boyee."

"Ha, don't worry. I intend to."

Angel turned to Raheim. "Holla before you leave, a'ight?"

"I will."

Angel joined Jazz on the dance floor.

Malice grinned. "Man, like I said, I was *just* talkin' about you."

"You were?"

"Yeah. We just got the new *Right On!*; Li'l Lou is on the

cover. I turn to the first page and there you are. I didn't know you was still modelin' for A-A."

Raheim didn't feel like goin' over that history—how All-American fired him in 1999 because he'd missed too many photo shoots and publicity events, but rehired him on probation (meaning more folks would see him in magazine and newspaper ads than in public forums) after the September 11 attacks because they wanted to put on a "united" front (they knew they couldn't truly reflect the diversity of America with a stable of white models and a single Negress)—so he gave him the very short story. "Yeah. But my contract is up in September."

"I ain't seen you in moons, yo." He half circled Raheim. "But I see you still got them hella-hiya moons in da back."

Raheim rolled his eyes.

Malice stood just inches from Raheim's face. "You been on the down-low for some time."

Raheim couldn't resist this one. He drew back a step. "*I* been on the down-low? *You* the one with the wife on the West Coast."

Given all the hype surrounding the "discovery" of down-low men, even boyz like Malice who might fall under that category and once embraced the label don't like being tagged with it now. He frowned. "Nigga, you know what I mean."

"And *you* know what *I* mean. Can't have nobody jumpin' outta bushes with a camera catchin' you comin' out of a spot like this."

"Some things never change. You still a funny mutha-fucka." His eyes darted up and down. "And you still a *phyne* mutha-fucka. You lookin' damn *jood*."

Raheim smiled—a little.

"You ain't gonna gimme no love, yo?" Malice groused.

"What?"

"You heard. You bein' chilly 'n' shit."

"No, I ain't."

"You are, too." He leaned back on the bar. He shook his head. "Nigga, don't tell me you still stewin' about that night wit' Da Camp."

"No, I ain't," Raheim lied.

"Yeah, right. You need to let that shit go, brutha. That shit happened, like, *moons* ago. Whatcha drinkin'?"

"I don't want a drink. I was about to leave when you came up."

"You can't go yet." He grabbed Raheim's arm.

Raheim glanced down; he shook his arm free. "Yeah, I can."

"C'mon, brutha, don't be like that. Just have one drink. *One* drink. So I can just look at your hella-hiya azz for a few more minutes before you break and leave a nigga cold."

Raheim's head was telling him HELL NO but his . . . well, *other* head was telling him HELL YEAH. And since it had been a jood six months since he had anyone up in his grill, he caved. "*One* drink. And then I'm outta here."

Mitchell was heading out of the bathroom and back to his seat when he passed two brothers screeching with delight at the bar. Their joy was directed at another brother, who had his back to Mitchell. And when Mitchell looked down at this brother's *back* . . . well, let's just say that he'd know that ass *anywhere*.

It was Montee. Montee Simms. Mitchell hadn't seen or spoken to him since that Sunday morning in 1995 when Montee dropped Mitchell off at the West Third and Sixth Avenue basketball court after their twenty-four-hour rendezvous. They'd met on the dance floor at a weekly party called Body & Soul and, after two weeks of "accidentally" running into each other in other locales, had a very brief but juicy dalliance while Raheim was in Hollywood making his first film. Since then, Montee has managed to have the kind of music career that many artists never get close to—and that's saying a lot, considering the fact that he's an openly bisexual performer.

You'd think that alone would've turned him into a media sensation. But Montee had someone else to thank for his big break . . .

The Gay Rapper.

Profiled anonymously in a fanzine called *One Nut Network*

in 1996, this brother sent the hip-hop world into a serious tizzy. Some refused to believe he existed (how could he, when *gay* and *hip-hop* are supposedly opposites in every sense of the word?). Others didn't want to believe he existed but knew that he could (but they would never admit that publicly). And there were those who knew he existed, but wished he'd just go away (this was a side of hip-hop they didn't want the world to know about). Wherever folks fell on the spectrum, everyone wanted to know who he was. So, a year and a half was spent trying to sniff him out—and *snuff* him out (after all, he was tarnishing the genre's image as the domain of only hard-core heteros, and more than a few allegedly straight Negroes boasted they'd eliminate him if they discovered his identity). One of the most vocal "homiesexual" hunters was Wendy Williams, a radio deejay in New York who spent countless hours on the air not only speculating about who the Gay Rapper could be, but who else in the industry might be down. Her riotous, reckless dust-ups caused so much noise that she was allegedly fired for throwing the names of some very popular and powerful acts into the "is he or ain't he?" hat.

But just when it seemed the controversy was puttering out, Montee poured more gas on the fire. When asked by a reporter from *USA Today* doing a short Q&A and review of his first CD if he knew who the Gay Rapper was, he replied without missing a beat: "*The* Gay Rapper? There's more than one and *I* should know—I've slept with a few of them."

The next thing you knew, he was on Wendy's show dishin' the dirt, and his single, "It Ain't the Same Old Song," started climbing the charts, eventually peaking at #2 R&B and #11 pop (it stalled in both positions for five weeks). The song eventually went gold and the album it was culled from, *Soul-full Sounds*, which included a cover of The Intruders' "I Wanna Know Your Name," did one better by going platinum

and earned him double Grammy, Soul Train, and Image
Award nominations. It was the last citation that caused a little
ruckus. After all, what kind of "image" could the NAACP be
supporting, argued some conservative members and religious
pundits, nominating an openly bisexual performer who was
unapologetic about his sinful, sexual exploits with other men?
But the Old School (not Old Skool) guard that pushed for his
nominations didn't care about who he slept with. As one told
Jet, "Too many of today's young artists sample the songs of
old with little regard for where the tunes and the artists that
recorded them were coming from. But he [Simms] is a true
musician who understands and appreciates that legacy. He
doesn't treat the classics as something to bastardize for a quick
hit." He didn't win any of the awards, but his commercial
success and critical recognition was a triumph not only for the
industry (more like a sideswipe, not a body blow, against
homo/biphobia) but for the various communities—bisexual,
Black and SGL, and white and gay—that claimed him (the
social group Bi Any Other Name selected him as their person
of the year, Gay Men of African Descent in New York hon-
ored him at their annual banquet, and he received the Gay
and Lesbian American Music Award/GLAMA for best male
vocalist and best new artist, even though he is neither gay
nor lesbian).

Montee wasn't stupid, though; he knew his fourteen minutes
of fame would fade quick. He was an aberration, and as soon as
the rumormongers and gossip hounds found a new topic to
milk, he'd be old news and all but forgotten. So he took advantage of his notoriety by dabbling in a lot of everything: writing,
producing, and arranging for other "neosoul" artists, such as
D'Angelo, Musiq, Maxwell, and Angie Stone; being a guest vocalist on CDs by Roy Hargrove and Kirk Whalum; showing up
as a guest V-jay on VH-1; doing jingles for Crest, JCPenney,

Mitsubishi, and Carnival Cruise Lines; performing for four months in a road company called *Soul Revue*, impersonating his idol, Sam Cooke; portraying a (what else?) bisexual college student on an episode of *Moesha*; and appearing in a Gap ad like his heroine, Me'shell NdegéOcello.

Most of his public appearances over the past few years as a singer have been split between gay and straight audiences who love his music and don't hold his being bisexual against him. (His Mother's Day and "Fellaz Only" Valentine's Day concerts are always sold out.) And in addition to playing for both groups, he's played *to* them: in late 2000, he released two versions of his sophomore CD, *On the Menu*—one for men, the other for women (a remake of DeBarge's "Who's Holding Donna Now?" was a top twenty pop and R&B hit; its B side was "Who's Holding Donny Now?"). The combined sales brought him another platinum record, and the male version swept the OutMusic Awards. It also didn't hurt that, around this time, Wendy and her ilk sought out his insight on down-low brothers. (He stopped the show on both BET's *Oh Drama!*, when he informed co-hostess Kym Whitley, who couldn't imagine "big, burly, butch men rolling around with each other," that "I'm quite sure there are big, burly, butch men who can't imagine rolling around with *you*"; and the syndicated *America's Black Forum*, where he told conservative commentator Armstrong Williams, "You profess to know a *whole* lot about gay men; sure you're not one of them?")

Instead of just tapping him on the shoulder, Mitchell decided to be a groupie. "Excuse me, Mr. Simms, but could I *please* have your autograph?" he squealed.

Montee turned around and a very, *very* wide grin formed across his face. *"Mitchell,"* he crooned, wrapping Mitchell up in his arms and hugging him so tight Mitchell had to gasp for air. He released Mitchell from the grip but not from his arms; they settled around Mitchell's waist. "I *can't* believe it."

"Believe it."

"*Damn.* I . . . I . . ."

"You never thought you'd see me again."

"No, I didn't. What are you doing here?"

"I'm out with the crew." He looked over to their table.

Montee focused on them. "Oh, your friends. Babyface, B.D., and . . ."

"Ha, you *better* remember the other's name. He believes he is *un*forgettable."

"Uh . . . Gene?"

"Right."

"Man, I just can't believe this. But I have to. I'm holding you."

And he continued to hold him as they gazed.

Montee took him in, hair to toe. "You look *so* good."

"So do you."

"How have you been?"

"Fine. And you?"

"Same. Can't complain. Your hair is *fly*."

"Thank you. I'd say the same, but . . ."

They laughed. Montee, who once sported an Afro, was now bald.

"How long have you been growing your locks?"

"About three and a half years. How long have you been skinned?"

"About a year now. I saw that gray hair comin' in and decided to cut it off at the pass."

"I'm sure you'd look even sexier with gray hair."

"Not as sexy as you."

Mitchell blushed.

Montee shook his head. "*Damn* . . . it is just *so* good to see you."

They gazed some more.

"Well," Mitchell began, glancing at the brothers Montee

had been conversing with before he interrupted them, "I don't want to keep you."

"Oh, no, don't go." He squeezed him a little tighter and drew him a little closer. "I was about to blow this joint in a minute. Have you eaten?"

"I have."

"Well, how about watching *me* eat? I know how much you enjoy to."

He has a jood memory...

"This'll give us a chance to catch up on the last eight years."

Actually it's been eight years, three months, and five days—but who's counting...?

"Sure, why not," Mitchell agreed.

"Great. I'll just wrap this up and meet you at your table in five minutes."

"Okay."

Montee wouldn't let him go.

"Uh, the only way you're going to meet me over at my table is if I am over there, too." Mitchell glanced down.

"*Oh.*" Montee reluctantly released him. "Sorry. See you in a bit."

Mitchell returned to the table and faced the third degree from both B.D. and Gene.

"See, you go to the restroom and end up in the arms of some man," Gene chastised.

"Oh, but it's not just some man, dearest—it's *Montee*," B.D. emphasized.

"He looks *jood*," remarked Babyface, leering at Montee (or, rather, at his ass).

"Uh-huh. And we know you are *not* talking about the cheeks on his *face*," quipped B.D.

"Ha, you know I ain't. That ass defies logic."

"*Oh?*" B.D. snapped.

"Yeah." Babyface pulled him closer, sliding his hands down to his rump. "But *yours* defies the laws of nature, physics, *and* gravity."

"*Oh, my Shnookums...*" B.D. cooed, wrapping his arms around his neck. They tongue-danced.

"*Yeesh,*" Gene shrieked, disgusted by the smooching. "Why don't you two take that shit home."

"That sounds like a *very* jood idea," agreed B.D., rubbing his man's nose with his own. "The youngun will be gone until Sunday night and *I* intend to take full advantage of that. Like Mz Ann Nesby, 'This weekend, I'll be makin' love to *my* man'."

"You know it," Babyface affirmed, snacking on his neck.

Gene cringed. His eyes then fell on Mitchell. "And it looks like someone else will be going buck wild this weekend—or, at least for one night."

"Are you still touring with Me'shell?" Mitchell asked Montee as they turned the corner at Greenwich Avenue and walked down Seventh Avenue.

"Yeah. I'm opening for her tomorrow night at B.B. King's spot at eight. Why don't you come and check us out? I can getcha a front-row-center seat like before."

"Just *a* seat. What if I wanted to bring someone?"

Montee stopped. "Now, you know I ain't inviting you and some other brother to come hear me sing to *you*."

Mitchell giggled. "I'd love to, but I'll be chaperoning a party."

"Oh? Is Gene havin' another one of his famous bashes?"

"No. It's my godson. He just turned fifteen."

"Mph. You gonna have your hands full."

"And *you've* certainly had *your* hands full, mister big-time producer. I *love* the songs you did with Carl, Joe, Donell, and Kelly. And I hear you're working with Alicia, Jagged Edge, Usher, *and* Jilly from Philly."

"Uh, yeah. Hmm . . ." Montee rubbed his chin with his right thumb. "You still stalkin' me, huh?"

They grinned.

"So, how *you* livin' these days? You the editor-in-chief of your own magazine yet?"

He remembered. . . . "No. But I may be soon. I got an offer today to helm a new Black magazine. They want to meet with me on Tuesday."

"That's great, Mitchell! What's it called?"

"Nothing yet. They say that's up to me."

"Wow. Have you made a decision yet?"

"No. I'm gonna see what they have to say next week."

"Good luck with that, man."

"Thanks."

"You still in Fort Greene?"

"Yeah. I bought a brownstone six years ago."

"Ah, we're both home owners. Your settlement must've come through."

He remembered that, too. . . . "It did."

"And you live in this big brownstone all by your little brown self?"

"No. With my daughter and—"

"*Your who?*" This time Montee stopped so cold in his tracks he almost tripped over his feet.

"My daughter."

"*You* . . . have a *daughter?*"

"Yes. Her name is Destiny. She's five."

"Hmmph . . . this is a conversation I *have* to have sitting down." Montee opened the door to Tiffany's.

Mitchell entered and couldn't believe his eyes. The place

had received a total makeover. Everything was different: the floors, the wallpaper, the booths, the tables, the chairs, the stools, the bar, the menus, even the silverware and table napkins. For a moment, he thought he was in the wrong restaurant. Time really does fly: he hadn't been there in close to a decade. One thing hadn't changed, though: the place was packed with SGL men (and a few women) of various shades of brown, kee-keeing away. He laughed to himself as they settled in a booth.

"What's funny?" Montee asked.

"Just thinking about my times here when it didn't look like a Four Seasons knockoff."

"I take it they were very good times."

"They were. I first ventured down here fifteen years ago. I didn't know how I managed to exist without it, and *couldn't* imagine not coming down every weekend. But now . . . my nights taking the homo stroll down Christopher Street, then eating here and watching the sun come up are over."

"But not your days of *being* a homo?" Montee chuckled.

"*Never.*"

The waiter took Montee's order and left. "So," Montee began, "I know you've got a wallet full of pictures of Destiny you can't wait to show me."

He did. There were twelve pictures arranged chronologically, beginning with her first day on earth in her hospital bin and ending with her Easter-egg hunting in Central Park two months ago.

Montee couldn't get over how beautiful she was. "She is a *baby doll.*"

"She is."

He studied father and daughter. "She's got your eyes."

"Well, she should."

"Are you telling me you *actually* . . ."

Mitchell laughed. He revealed how she was conceived.

"Damn," Montee said, as he chomped down on his cheese-burger and fries. "I thought you fathering her was wild, but that story is even wilder."

"And why is it so hard to believe that *I* could have fath-ered her?"

Montee didn't miss a beat. "If the phrase *strictly dickly* was in the dictionary, *your* picture would be next to it."

"Yes. But as a wise man once explained to me, 'Just because someone is oriented toward one sex does not mean they cannot be attracted to or be intimate with the other.' "

It took a few seconds, but it registered: *he* had said that. "What are you, an FBI agent?"

Mitchell chuckled.

"So, you're raising a daughter."

"And my godson, Errol."

"The fifteen-year-old having the birthday party?"

"Yes."

"How did he come to be with you?"

Mitchell gave his stock answer. "Since I live two blocks from his high school, his mother and father felt it was best he live with me."

"And . . . you're raising them alone?"

"I am."

"Ah . . . so, that brother you were with when we met . . ."

"We're . . . no longer together." *I haven't said that out loud in some time . . . feels like the first time.*

"Did you tell him about us?"

"I did. But we didn't break up because of you."

"Ah. How long has it been?"

"Close to four years."

"So, what happened between you two?"

Mitchell gave him a very abbreviated version of the

breakup. By the end of that story, they were sharing a slice of strawberry cheesecake.

"Do you two still talk?"

"Like twice a month. Mostly about Errol."

"Are you seeing anyone now?"

Mitchell knew he'd get around to asking that. "No. Looking after a teenager and a kindergartner doesn't leave much time for a social life."

"Even more reason for you to have one. When's the last time you had any?"

"Now, *that* is *none* of your business."

"That long, huh?"

Mitchell hesitated. "It's been a year."

"Who was he?"

He told him about Vinton Woodson, the contractor who redesigned and rebuilt his brownstone (built in 1792, it had been abandoned for thirty-five years until, through a neighborhood revitalization program, Mitchell purchsed the unit from the city for ten thousand dollars). Mitchell ran into Vinton at Dayo's in July 2001, and they dated for a year.

"Was that your longest relationship since . . . ?"

"Yes."

"Why did it end?"

"He wanted something more permanent."

"And you didn't?"

"I . . . I just wasn't sure if I wanted it with him."

"What was wrong with him?"

"Nothing."

"Then what was wrong with *you*?"

"Nothing. I just realized I was with him because he reminded me of my ex."

"Mmm. Does ol' boyee know he's got you strung out like this?"

"He doesn't have me strung out."

"What would you call it?"

Mitchell searched for an answer. "I still have feelings for him."

"Yeah, *strong* feelings."

Mitchell turned the tables. "Are *you* seeing anyone, socially or sexually?"

That was another Montee-ism being thrown back at him. "You got a good memory. I'm not at the moment, socially or sexually."

"I heard through the grapevyne you're seeing Bill-E." Bill-E is a new singer on the scene, a high-yellow Tyrese from Denver whose debut Montee coproduced. Like Montee, Bill-E is bow-legged and has a booty way out to *there*. Montee, who is knockin' on forty, is twice his age.

Montee frowned. "Where you hear that?"

"My sources."

"Who?"

"They're *my* sources; if I told you who they were, then they'd be *yours*."

"Well, as the white men in dark blue suits from Enron and WorldCom told America: 'On the advice of my attorney I invoke my Fifth Amendment privilege to respectfully refuse to answer questions on the grounds that they may incriminate me.' "

Mitchell then went in for the kill. "What about Noble?" Noble is a rap artist Montee was kickin' it with when they met.

To Mitchell's surprise, he was willing to talk about him. "We haven't been . . . together since the beginning of '96. When I came out swingin' in that *Source* interview, he was on that month's cover. So I'm sure he was glad what we had ended long before then."

"I'm glad you went there in that interview. And that you shut down Miss Conflama on *Oh Drama!*"

Montee rolled his eyes. "Oh, please, I'm tryin' to forget that mess!"

"And that you put Arm*wrong* in his place."

"Somebody needed to. He's such a moron. Not to mention bi-phobic and homophobic."

"Indeed. You deserved all the attention you got. It's just too bad you got it for the wrong reasons."

"Uh . . . do you still respect me?"

"Of course I do. Why wouldn't I?"

"You know . . . fanning the 'who is the Gay Rapper?' flames."

"You didn't fan the flames; you tried to blow the smoke in another direction. You were the only voice of reason during the whole episode. Besides, if anybody should be able to exploit such a phantom concept, why shouldn't it be a bisexual singer who knows firsthand who is gay in hip-hop?"

"Well, thanks. I knew we could juice it, the *right* way. Without the publicist's knowing it, I had an intern add the line 'Mr. Simms, who has had relationships with both men and women' to the press release. The very next day, we were getting calls, and they were all related to that."

"I'm sure the record company wasn't pleased."

"Nope. They were ready to pull the single and the CD and cancel the contract, arguing that I had breached the agreement since I signed on as a 'straight' artist."

"No, you didn't. They just *assumed* you were."

"*See*. They couldn't go into a court of law and argue that I misrepresented myself, since no one ever asked me the question, and there's no clause stating that. But they changed their tune when *Soul-full Sounds* started flying off the shelves."

"But they still dropped you."

"Yeah. With the second CD, they wanted me to be quiet about it, as if people would forget—and *I* would forget. They wanted me to sign a statement saying that I would not talk about it in interviews."

"You're kidding!"

"Nope. So we agreed it'd be best to part ways. I went right to work incorporating FoReal, hiring a small staff, and roping a distributor."

"I know you said you wanted to do that. I was so happy to hear you did."

"It's no big deal. Everybody and their aunt has their own record label these days."

"But they all don't have the kind of vision or talent you do. And I don't know of any other out acts who do gay and straight versions of their songs."

"As you know, flattery gets you *everywhere* with me." Montee winked.

Mitchell blushed then frowned. "Did you experience a backlash from others in the industry?"

"*Did?* I still *do*. I knew going in that I'd lose a few friends and gain some enemies. But I'm not bothered by the cold shoulder. I *am* bothered by the hypocrisy of some who don't wanna be friendly with me in public but try to get friendly with me at the after party . . ."

"*Or,* in the hotel lobby . . . ?"

"Right."

"Why don't you just blow their cover?"

"They just ain't in the space to do what I'm doin', and that's okay. But if they get stupid and start goin' off on some homo or biphobic rant, the whole world will know when, where, and *how* they sucked my dick and spread them cheeks."

"Mmm. Since you brought *that* up: I loved how you spread *yours* in *Playgirl*." When he was still *the* talk of the industry, Montee posed for the magazine. While there weren't any frontal nude shots (although his hard-on could be seen through the mesh wrap that draped him), there were plenty of his bare bootay.

Montee gushed. "Folks *still* bring it to events for me to

sign. I never would've thought so many brothers read that magazine."

"Ha, they weren't *reading* the magazine!"

They cracked up.

"Do you think other acts will follow your lead?"

"Posing in *Playgirl*?"

"No, silly. Being out."

"I hope so. But folks act like I'm the only one. There are many out artists; they just haven't gotten the press I have. But the time is ripe for a brother in hip-hop who has proven he's got skills to just break out. Hell, the world's most popular rap artist is a white boy and the most popular golfer is a brother. *Anything* is possible." Montee pointed to Mitchell. "*You* could follow my lead."

"Me?"

"Yeah, you. Have you been singing?"

"Just for Destiny."

"Ah. What do you sing for her?"

"Number one on her list is 'Now I Know My ABC's,' by Patti LaBelle."

"From when she was on *Sesame Street*?"

"Yes. Then there are nursery rhymes, Christmas carols, songs from *The Wiz* and *Willy Wonka*. They're her favorite movies."

"Mmm. I'm sure she loves to hear her daddy sing."

"She does."

"*I'd* love to hear her daddy sing."

"Now?"

"Not now. After we get out of here."

Hmm . . . "And just *where* would this performance take place?"

Montee thought about it. "How about the Monster? They have a piano."

"Uh-huh, which someone is *paid* to play."

"So, I'll talk to the manager."

"He won't let you play. He probably doesn't know who you are."

"Then it's time he did. Come on, for old time's sake. *Please?*"

Some things never change: the man knew how to beg—and knew that it worked.

Montee bypassed the manager and just slipped Dalton, the piano man, fifty dollars to take his stool during his half-hour break. Some of the bar's patrons were men of color, but Mitchell still had his doubts.

"Maybe we shouldn't do this."

"Why not? You got cold feet?"

"No. I just don't want to humiliate myself."

"And how could you humiliate yourself with *me* on the keys?"

"Well, this *is* the Monster. They like to hear stuff by Barbra and Judy."

"Don't sweat it. Even if they don't appreciate what we do, *we* will." He motioned for Mitchell to sit next to him on his left; Mitchell did. Montee began to play.

Mitchell (and many of those in the bar) recognized the song immediately. He couldn't believe Montee had chosen this song. *Does he expect me to sing it with him?*

When Montee got to Miss Ross's part, he nudged Mitchell.

" 'My first love?' " Mitchell sang as a question but on key. They laughed.

And those listening laughed—not at them, but with them.

After they harmonized the chorus for the final time, the crowd's reaction reminded Mitchell of that scene in *Coal Miner's Daughter* when Loretta Lynn (aka Sissy Spacek) performs for the first time at a honky-tonk. Petrified and unsure, she does her thing and the folks love her so much they want her to do another song.

"Woof woof woof!" hooted a Bla-tino duo sitting just two feet from them.

"Y'all betta sang!" screamed a fifty something brother, clapping furiously.

"Encore, encore!" shouted a white drag queen, who favored Gwen Stefani.

"Thanks so much." Montee grinned, giving Mitchell an *I-told-you-so* glance. "I'm Montee, and this is Mitchell."

Mitchell acknowledged the audience by slightly bowing his head.

"Dalton has graciously allowed us to do an intermission set. So we're gonna do a few more selections and hope that you enjoy them."

Those few more selections were also duets from the eighties: Barbra & Barry's "Guilty," Roberta & Peabo's "Tonight, I Celebrate My Love," Patti & James's "Baby, Come to Me," Aretha & George's "I Knew You Were Waiting (For Me)," and Michael & Paul's "The Girl Is Mine," on which the "girl" became a "boy" and they did an ad-lib that brought down the house . . .

"You know, Montee?"

"Yeah, Mitch?"

"You just need to hang it up—and *zip* it up. The boy belongs to *me*."

"That's not what he told me last night."

"Uh-huh. He must've mumbled it after his third or fourth screwdriver."

"As a matter of fact, it was after the third or fourth time I screwed him *with* my driver!"

"It took you *that* many tries to get it right? It only took one bangin' from me and he was *sangin'* . . ." And Mitchell hit an octave that caused a glass on a nearby table to shatter— and the entire bar (which now included many of the patrons who had been on the dance floor, which is on the lower level) exploded in hysterical laughter that lasted several minutes.

The audience begged for one more song, and Mitchell wasn't the least bit surprised that Montee chose a tune by his favorite songwriters: Ashford & Simpson. Folks shouted the hook to "Solid" so loudly that a police officer warned management about the noise.

They took their bows to a foot-stomping standing ovation. They received many drinks and indecent proposals, including two propositions to engage in a ménage à trois. And the manager pleaded with them to do an hour show every Friday night. They turned down all these offers, but not the $226 in tips that filled two large beer mugs (this tally, as well as the adulation they received, made Dalton fume). Mitchell collected and counted it; Montee told him to keep it.

"*You* are a *genius*," Mitchell proclaimed as they exited the bar, arm in arm.

"I don't know about that . . ." Montee gushed.

"You knew *just* what to play. How were you able to read them so well?"

"I figured we couldn't go wrong starting out with 'Endless Love.' It might be one of the schmaltziest songs ever recorded, but it's a song everybody loves—even if they're reluctant to admit it. We gave it the twist it needed. I'm sure there are many men who have played it, sang it for their boyfriends. But to see two men sing it in public?"

"Yeah, that clinched it."

"The songs were right. But my duet partner made it *all* right."

Mitchell grinned. "You took a big gamble on me. I might not have known the words to any of those songs. Or I could've known but froze up."

"Wasn't gonna happen. I had faith in you—and in us. And

they're right: we *should* record a CD. Hell, we performed half the album tonight. And, as you saw, it would be a hit."

"I guess so. And what would we call ourselves?"

Montee considered it. "M&M, what else?"

"The Mars company will have a *big* problem with that."

"Ha, let 'em sue a tiny record label in Georgia. You know how much attention we'll get—and how many copies we'll sell then?"

Mitchell sighed a smile. "Thanks."

"For what?"

"For this. I needed it. I haven't done something impulsive like it in so long. It was frightening but fun."

"I'm glad. If you really wanna get wild, we can head over to this karaoke drag bar on Third and Sixteenth." Montee looked at his watch. "Miss Ross should be hitting the stage in about five minutes."

"Uh, I'd love to but I have a very busy day tomorrow."

"But it's only two."

"Which means I've already missed four hours of the sleep I'm used to getting. I have a house to get in order and food to prepare."

"Uh, okay. Let me give you a lift. My car is parked on the next street."

"What happened to your motorcycle?"

"She's in Atlanta. I drive to most of my events, unless I'm going to Cali."

"Ah. What kind of car?"

"An Acura."

"What, no Mercedes?"

"*Hell* no."

Mitchell chuckled. "An Acura isn't exactly the type of vehicle one would expect a big-time producer to drive."

"Please, I don't plan on goin' broke, spending all my green on luxury cars and jewelry. So, how 'bout it?"

"I'd appreciate it. Thanks."

"But, like a cabbie, *I* expect a tip."

"Oh? A cabbie usually gets fifty cents."

"I'll take fifty *smacks* instead."

"Ha, where?"

Montee's eyebrows rose. "Twenty-five on the lips—and twenty-five below the *hips*!"

J ust like before, it all started with one drink—and just like before, that was one drink too many.

That first drink loosened Raheim up. He got tired of listening to Malice yak about his kids (their joint eight-figure deal with Sony, their clothing lines, and the mini-mansions built for them on their parents' property) and started bragging about his own being a genius.

The second drink, to Malice's delight, got Raheim *loose*. Malice always picked the right time to lean forward, lean in, lean on him, lean against him—and Raheim welcomed it (Raheim *was* still attracted to him; Malice had a little gut, but the rest of the body was still tight and stacked, particularly that azz). Malice asked him to dance, and within a half hour, both were bare-chested and bumpin' with a vengeance on the floor. After three hours of that, they both knew it was time to take it to the head—literally.

Raheim was a little drunk (if one can be a *little* drunk) and Malice was a lotta drunk—but not *that* drunk that he forgot what hotel and which room he was in. His room door hadn't closed when he was on his knees unzipping Raheim's fly and gobblin' him up.

"*Day-um,*" Raheim groaned, trying to keep his balance. After getting steady, Raheim got *heady*. It felt *so* jood to have someone's mouth wrapped around his dick, and what a skillful mouth it was: Malice's lips weren't made to just suck dick but inhale it. His lips are legendary: he's gone down on *many* in the hip-hop world, including a few record execs. (One of those encounters allegedly happened in a first-class airplane lavatory.) And he could multitask: As he gave Raheim some jood head he pulled down Raheim's jeans and bikini briefs, and worked off his own white sweatpants and stroked his own dick.

After a few more minutes of deep-throatin', Malice knew Raheim was on the verge of a volcanic eruption and pulled back. "Nah, I ain't about to have you cummin' yet. I want ya to get jizzy up in this." He hopped across the room and fell onto his back on the bed, raising his legs up and tossing his bright orange G-string onto the bureau.

"C'mon, nigga, you know you wanna taste that azz." He gloated, pointing the bottom of his Timbs to the ceiling and spreading his cheeks.

Raheim pushed Malice's knees farther into his chest and pushed his face into Malice's crack.

"*Yeah, nigga, lick it wicked,*" Malice cooed.

After Raheim licked it wicked for a while, Malice flipped over on all fours, his azz pointed straight at Raheim, and threw a condom between his legs that landed at the edge of the bed. "Come on, nigga, you know you wanna nail that azz."

Raheim ripped it open and rolled it down, lubed him up with his middle finger, and drove right on in.

"*Ooh, yeah, crank it up while I yank it up,*" Malice demanded.

On every crank, Malice yanked his own dick. And as Raheim went in deeper, Malice's grunts got louder and longer and lighter, his voice moving from baritone to falsetto. He was all in it and all into it.

Raheim was in it—but he wasn't *in*to it. He was up in it—but he wasn't up *in*to it. And it was feelin' real jood; in fact, *bet-*

ter than jood. But it's like his pops told him: "Just 'cause it's jood *to* ya don't mean it's jood *for* ya." He felt like he was taking a step back *in* Malice's back. Malice made him weak in the knees, but that didn't mean he had to become weak and fall for his game again. He couldn't blame the alcohol; he'd made a conscious decision to allow himself to be seduced. As he learned while in the twelve-step recovery program, there are just some behaviors and people you have to delete from your life, or else you'll be regressing and not progressing. He had to close the chapter on Malice—and this was *not* the way to do it. He didn't belong here and he didn't belong with Malice, *anywhere*.

So, he did something he's *never* done before: right smack dab in the middle of bangin' some bootay, he slid out, slid off the condom, and slid into his underwear.

The azz still twirlin' in sync, Malice snapped his head back, looking at Raheim in utter disbelief. "*Nigga*, what the *fuck's* goin' on?"

"I'm outta here."

"*What?*"

"I don't wanna no more."

Malice was . . . well, insulted *and* mortified—and he had no problem letting Raheim know it . . .

"*Nigga*, what the *fuck* you mean, 'I don't wanna?' *You don't wanna?* What kinda *fuckin'* shit is that? How you *not* gonna want *this?* You know how many niggas want a piece of this? You know how many niggas want just a little *taste* of this? You know how many niggas been beggin' to get all hella up in this? Shit, that list would be bigger than a fuckin' phone book. *And you don't want it?* See, I shoulda known. Your *punk* azz been runnin' away from it for years. Always comin' up with some ty-ad fuckin' excuse not to. Like, *I'm in love.* Nigga, who the *fuck* would love *yo'* triflin' azz? Ya can't handle it and ya could never handle it. After all these fuckin' years, and ya *still* don't know what the fuck to do. You *wish* you could fuck like a real nigga, yo. You'd lose your fuckin' mind *up in here, up in here. God-day-um.* I can't believe I wasted all this *fuckin'* time sweatin' yo' punk azz. And you got all that dick goin' to waste— and it *is* goin' to waste, mutha-fucka, if it ain't fucked *this* azz. So go on, get the *fuck* out. No wonder yo' sorry azz got caught up gamin'; ya gotta know how to *play* the game, and you can't. But, yo, make sure you take one good long look at *this* 'cause you ain't *never* gonna see or have some azz like this again, for the rest of your sorry-azz life. Memorize it, mutha-fucka, 'cuz you ain't never gonna forget it, you ain't never gonna get it— and you *will* regret it."

There was a lot Raheim wanted to rattle off, too. But Malice's bitchin' out like Grace Jones in *Boomerang* was just the revenge he needed. He didn't bust a nut, but you'd think he had given the grin on his face.

Montee pulled into a parking space across the street from Mitchell's home.

"Thanks for the lift."

"You're more than welcome."

"It . . . it's been a good night."

"Don't you mean *jood*?"

They laughed.

"Yes, jood," Mitchell agreed.

"It can be an even jood*er* morning, if that's a word."

"It *is* the morning."

"You know what I mean."

"Yes, I do. And I'm sure it could be. I'd like to . . ."

"But?"

"I can't."

"Yes, you can."

"Let me put it this way: My body might be here with you . . ."

This was one lyric Montee didn't have fun finishing with him. ". . . but your mind would be on the other side of town."

Mitchell nodded.

"Well, it ain't really the body I'm interested in, it's da booty."

Mitchell laughed.

Montee shrugged. "If it won't bother me . . ."

"Yes, it would."

He sat back and huffed. "Yeah. It would. I tell you, that brother is *always* messin' up my plans. Well . . . instead of gettin' our freak on, how about we get our *friend* on? You look like you could use a chest to lay your head on."

Mitchell smiled. "That, I'd like."

"And I think it's *my* turn to fix breakfast."

"And I'd *really* like that."

saturday,
june 7, 2003

They decided to live together because they had to. Now they live together because they want to.

His father is the *last* person Raheim ever thought he'd be splitting the bills with. Actually, *splitting the bills* is the wrong phrase to describe their living arrangement: his father covers and writes all the checks each month for the two bedroom co-op in Jersey City (the mortgage, electric, gas, phone, and cable are all in his name). When he saw that his son was having an emotional meltdown in the summer of '99, Mr. Rivers insisted that Raheim come live with him; after being an alcoholic for much of his twenties and thirties, he knew how tough conquering an addiction and getting one's life back on track could be. Raheim appreciated the offer but was a little suspicious; was this his father's way of making up for the fact that he stepped out on him when he was a kid? There had been other attempts over the last decade since he resurfaced, starting with the invite he and Li'l Brotha Man received to attend the Million Man March (since they were going anyway, Raheim accepted; it would be, as his father told him later that night, the very best moment of his life, having his son with him to share that special day and finally meeting his grandson). And while Raheim did reach out to him that night in that hotel room because he needed him, he didn't believe he needed him *that* much. But he had to reconsider that position after he had a re- lapse (after his sixth Gamblers Anonymous meeting, he thought he had it beat and knew he could walk into a casino and not be tempted—and nearly had another Flintstone fit when he was). Also, because he was facing a mile-high stack of gambling debts, credit-card bills, and default notices (he had to sell the Jeep, the jewelry, and his overpriced fashions) and had been evicted from his three-bedroom apartment in Harlem (he was late with or had not paid his rent at all for six months), he accepted since his father only expected him to chip in for food and other incidentals.

After he moved in, though, Raheim learned there were a few other things expected of him. Since his father would be doing all of the cooking, Raheim had to do the dishes (as well as take out the trash). Because his father sometimes worked double shifts as a tollbooth clerk at the Holland Tunnel and had so few clothes to clean (the man hadn't purchased a new pair of jeans in ten years and still wore a very faded and tattered Kareem Abdul-Jabbar T-shirt), Raheim was on laundry duty. He was also responsible for dusting and polishing the furniture, sweeping and mopping the floors, and cleaning the bathroom.

And then there was "the check-in": if Raheim was out late or planned on not coming home, he'd have to call to let him know. Naturally, Raheim balked: even if the man was his fa- ther, that didn't give him the right to know where he was, who he was with, what he was doing, and when he'd be home. After all . . .

"I'm a grown man," he defiantly argued.

His father laughed. "You ain't a grown man until you reach your thirties—and by that time you'll wish you *weren't*." Be- fore Raheim could recover from that blow, he hit him with an- other one: "I know you can do the right thing—but you gotta show you can be trusted to do it."

"So, you don't trust me?"

"Of course I do. If I didn't, I wouldn't have let you move in here. You could rob me blind, put me in the hole. But that's a chance I'm willing to take. The real question is, can you trust yourself?"

Jood question. His life had been out of sync the past four years and he had already slipped once on the road to recovery. So, even though the check-in and household chores initially made him feel like a teenager, he realized they were for his own jood, his father's way of keeping an eye out and providing him with some structure and stability. All his life he'd been carrying the weight himself, unwilling to let others help. Everybody needs a safe place to fall, where they can just be without judgment, a world away from the world that hasn't been patient with or kind to them—and the person who *was* that soft place for Raheim, he pushed away.

So while his father hadn't raised Raheim, he now stepped in to raise him *up*.

Raheim had kept him at a yard's distance since he popped back up nine years ago, but that wall came crumbling down during the almost four years they've been housemates. He's become a papa's boy—and he's proud of it. He's enjoyed living under the same roof and, in some ways, having the kind of relationship with his father he didn't have growing up. But he knows their being roomies will have to end, sooner rather than later. As his father has been hinting over the past year, "Now that you're in your thirties, you're officially a grown man—which means you've *out*grown me." Being a grown man means you have to be, not act, grown—and he sees that he was indeed acting the role over the past decade. After turning eighteen, he (like so many other young men) tripped into and stumbled through his twenties—and much of that tripping and stumbling was due to being hardheaded. He's finally grown up, thanks to his father, and although he hasn't made any announcement or started looking for a place of his own, he knows that has to be his next step. He can empathize with those adult children who find themselves back at Mom and Dad's doorstep after a divorce, losing a job, or out of plain homesickness.

Saturday morning has become their time to catch up. When Raheim emerged from the bathroom in green BVDs and a white tank, he walked toward the kitchen and found his father (also in green BVDs and a white tank; yup, they're dressing alike) standing over the stove, mixing a bowl of oatmeal.

The elder Rivers smiled. "Well . . . jood mornin', son."

"Jood mornin', Pop." Raheim took the orange juice out of the refrigerator.

"I was happy to see you weren't home when I got in last night. Hot date?"

Raheim filled their glasses, which were already on the table. "Not really."

"Not really? That means it started out red-hot and turned ice-cold."

He ain't lyin'. . .

He turned the eye under the pot off. "It happens—especially when you been off the market."

Raheim sat down at the dinette table. "Off the market?"

"Yeah. Something's wrong when your father dates more than you do." He poured them both some coffee in their favorite mugs (Raheim's from Gladys & Ron's Chicken & Waffles in Atlanta, his father's from the Professional Bowling League of America). He placed the coffeepot back on its holder. "So, who is he?"

Raheim grinned. There was a time when his father couldn't (or wouldn't) acknowledge that his son slept with men. And, like other fathers, he blamed himself . . .

It's my fault.

Why would you think that?

Because . . . I wasn't around.

If that was the case, a lot more bruthas out here would be.

But ... how did it happen?

How?

Yeah. Did somebody do somethin' to you?

No.

You sure? If so, you can tell me. You can tell me anything.

Pop, nobody did anything to me.

But something must have happened for it to ... happen.

It didn't just happen, and it didn't happen because something didn't happen. It just is. I guess I always knew.

You did?

Yeah.

When?

Uh, since I was a kid.

You mean, even when I was around?

Yeah.

But ... how did you know?

I was feelin' the same way about girls I was about boys.

Ah. Do you still have feelings for both?

I haven't been with a female in some time but ... I still have feelings for 'em.

His father took this disclosure as a sign of hope, and over the next three months tried to hook his son up with every attractive and available twentysomething sister he came across. His attempts failed, and not just because Raheim wasn't interested: many of those he approached believed the elder Rivers was using his son to get a date for himself. It wasn't until Raheim went out with the *brother* of one of these women that his father realized his efforts were in vain. He has, in his own way, come to accept who his son is—that he inquires about and is genuinely interested in Raheim's love life is proof.

"This brutha I ... met years ago," Raheim revealed.

"Mmm ... a booty call?"

"Pop!"

"I've had a few booty calls in my lifetime, too, ya know? Hey, whatever it takes so you don't lose your groove."

"*Lose* it? Ain't no way."

"Ah, spoken like a true Rivers man. Our rivers run *deep*."

They laughed.

He placed a bowl of cinnamon oatmeal and a plate of turkey sausage and scrambled eggs with cheese in front of him.

Raheim's eyes danced. "Thanks."

His father chuckled. "Welcome." He filled his own bowl.

"How was *your* date last night, Pop?"

"*Very* jood."

"And how was Millie?"

"As *nasty* as she wanted to be."

"And you loved every minute of it."

"You know I did. Thanks again for the tickets, son."

"You welcome."

"Like Al Sharpton, Millie is one person you don't wanna cross. 'Cause if you do, *he'll* be walkin' and *she'll* be talkin'."

"Did Amelia enjoy the concert?" Amelia is his girlfriend; they've been seeing each other for a year. At forty-one, she's a decade younger than him.

"She did."

"I still can't believe she never heard of Millie Jackson."

"She heard of her, she just never *heard* her before."

"Ha, then she got a earful last night."

"Yeah. She kept sayin' Millie reminded her of Lil' Kim. You know I ain't know who she was talkin' about."

"Yeah, I know." Raheim snickered under his breath.

"So on our drive back to Jersey she played a few of her songs. I was like, *damn!* Millie got a mouth, but that girl got *mouth*. She said things Millie probably wishes she coulda put on wax back in the day."

"I think they did a commercial together a few years ago."

"For who—*Hustler*?"

They laughed.

The elder Rivers sat down, prayed silently over his food, and was about to pick up the salt when Raheim swiped it. His father huffed. "A little sprinkle ain't gonna hurt me, son." His blood pressure is up, so he has to watch his intake.

"Like you know how to sprinkle on a little?"

His father frowned. He doubled up on the pepper instead. "I'm goin' food shoppin' later on. You need somethin'?"

"Nah. What you cookin' tomorrow?"

"I ain't cookin' nothin'. Amelia will be. I'll be too busy keepin' my eye focused on the prize."

"Oh, yeah. You got practice today?" He's a member of the Mellow Fellows, a bowling team. They'll be competing in the Jersey City Bowling League's quarter finals tomorrow.

"Son, you know your father don't need to practice. But my *teammates* . . . ?"

Raheim chuckled.

"I'll be watchin' *them* practice to make sure practice *does* make perfect."

"What was your average last week?"

"One-ninety."

"Wow, Pop. Y'all should win."

"We better. I'm not losin' three years in a row."

"Is Amelia gonna be cheerin' you on?"

"Yeah. You know the fellas love her to death—and the women can't stand her. They just hatin'. She younger, prettier, *and* smarter."

"And you never let 'em forget it."

"You know it. Uh, you got my jersey?"

If he can't find it in his own closet, it's in Raheim's. "Yeah. I'm gonna—"

"—wash it today, yeah, I heard that before. You got a full day—*and* night."

"I'll do it right after breakfast."

"You know that laundry room is always packed on a Saturday."

"If it is, I'll just head to the one around the corner."

"And you'll be waiting for a washer and a dryer all day, there, too."

"I'll get it done before the tournament tomorrow."

"Okay."

Raheim turned on *Soul Train*. They finished the rest of the meal in silence, watching Heather Headley belt out "I Wish I Wasn't."

Raheim slurped up the rest of his oatmeal. "That was *so* jood, Pop."

"Glad you enjoyed it."

Raheim sighed heavily. He peered at his father.

The elder Rivers was familiar with that pitiful look. "Okay, okay, *okay*: I'll do the dishes and you get the laundry done, *to-day*."

"Thanks, Pop." Raheim beamed. "I'll get to it right now."

Montee woke Mitchell up by ringing his bell.

It's a facsimile of the Liberty Bell that Mitchell purchased years ago when he visited Philadelphia. It had come in handy last November when Destiny caught a bug; bedridden for a couple of days, she'd ring it when she needed her father.

He opened his eyes and sat up as Montee put down the tray. On one plate was a stack of syrup-soaked blueberry pancakes, surrounded by six strips of bacon; on the other, an omelet with onions and green peppers. There was also a bowl of grapes and glasses of orange juice and ice water.

"Good morning," Montee sang.

"Good morning."

"A promise is a promise." He took the linen napkin folded across his arm and draped it across Mitchell's thighs. He then inched the tray up.

"Thank you so much. What a delicious-looking spread. I see you didn't have a problem finding anything."

"Not at all."

Mitchell pointed to the thin white vase, which had a few daisies in it. "Did you get them from Destiny's garden?"

"Destiny's garden?"

"Yes, she has her own little area in the backyard."

"Ah. I guess I did. I hope she won't mind."

"I'm sure she won't. Aren't you going to join me?"

"Of course I am." He eased onto the other side of the bed, lying on his right side with his head propped up on his bent right arm. He opened his mouth.

"You expect me to feed you?"

"*Hell* yeah. That's one of the rewards of being the chef."

Mitchell obliged. He let him have the first taste.

"This is some palace you live in," Montee complimented.

"It's not a palace."

"How many square feet is it?"

"Six thousand two hundred and seventy-five."

"You don't call *that* a palace? In some parts, this would be considered an estate."

Mitchell shrugged.

"You clean this place yourself?"

"Yes."

"I hate to clean, so I have a maid come in once a month. You'd need one once a *week* up in here."

"I couldn't have someone else do it. I enjoy the sweeping and the mopping and the dusting. It's therapy for me."

"You can tell this is your house; it has a very calm, welcoming spirit. You've been doin' a lot of livin' up in here—but clearly not a lot of *lovin'*."

Mitchell didn't want to go there with him, so . . . "You know, I always wanted to know something. It isn't on your Web site and I don't think you ever addressed it in interviews. Or maybe you were never asked."

"What?"

"How did you get the nickname Montee?"

"Ah. My little sister could never say Montgomery. She'd always chop it. Mon-ty. Pretty soon, everyone was calling me Monty."

"But you dropped the *Y* and added two *E*s?"

"Yeah. It didn't look right on paper, so I knew it wouldn't look right on a marquee. Uh, there's something *I* always wanted to know all these years, too."

"Oh? What?"

"Did you . . . think about me, at all?"

"You crossed my mind—once or twice." Mitchell laughed.

Montee wasn't laughing. "I thought you forgot about me."

"Forgot about you?" Mitchell pushed the tray forward and scooted out of bed. He retrieved a photo album from inside one of the entertainment-center compartments. He placed it in Montee's hands.

Montee opened it. It was a clip portfolio, documenting his career: CD and concert reviews, profiles, flyers, ads, "mentions" in trend stories and gossip columns. And tucked in the very back was that issue of *Playgirl.*

"Montgomery 'Montee' Simms, this is your life," Mitchell announced.

"*Damn.* You got stuff in here I never knew about. *You* shoulda been my publicist." Montee finally noticed something about one of the bylines. He looked up at Mitchell, wide-eyed. "*You're* MC."

Mitchell raised his right hand. "Guilty."

"Why didn't you just use your full name?"

"I knew that, one day, we'd reunite and I'd reveal it. Besides, I didn't want you to think I was stalking you."

"Ha, too late." He thumbed through a few more pages. "Wow. I guess you didn't forget about me."

"How could I? You served me some of the very best breakfast booty I ever had." He smacked him on his ass.

"And you scooped it up like nobody ever did before," Montee moaned. "Uh . . . would you like some for old time's sake?"

Mitchell licked his lips. "Breakfast wouldn't be the same without it."

———————

Montee squeezed him tight. "Sade said it's never as good as the first time. She lied."

They laughed. They were soaking in the master garden tub, Mitchell between Montee's legs.

Mitchell shifted to face him. "You were as tasty as ever."

"So were you."

"And *freaky* as ever."

"Ditto."

"And, you broke your rule, *again*."

"Say what?"

"No hanky-panky, no spanky-spanky, remember?"

"*I* broke it? I think I had some help."

"It was *your* rule, not *mine*."

"Uh-huh. Well, rules are made to be broken; at least mine are, by me."

"Don't tell me: Bette Davis in *Death on the Nile*, right?"

"Yeah. How you know?"

"They showed it the other night on AMC."

"Did you enjoy it?"

"It was okay. The book was better."

"Ain't it always?"

"Mmm-hmm. I take it you're still a mystery buff . . . ?"

"Yup. When I'm on the road, I take an audiovox with me so I can watch my favorite episodes of *Columbo*. I wish they'd release 'em on DVD. I've had to rerecord them all. The tapes were old and I wore them out."

"Uh-huh. Just like me—but in a *jood* way."

"You know it. Uh, where does that word come from, anyway?"

I might as well tell him . . . "My ex."

"You mean *the* ex?"

"Yes, *the* ex."

"Ah. Not only does he have *jood* taste, he's a clever brother. I may have to use that word in a song."

"If you do, I expect royalties."

"Huh?"

"After all, you never would've known about it if you hadn't met me."

"True. How you wanna be paid: cold cash or coochie coupon?"

"Hmm ... I can't have both?"

"Damn, you greedy."

"*And,* I want a dedication in the liner notes."

"*And* pushy. We'll discuss those details if and when it happens. Ya know ... I *did* dedicate a song to you on the last CD."

"What song?"

" 'Early E'vry Midnite.' "

Mitchell had wanted to assume the song referred to him but he might not have been *that* Mitchell. He was glad to find out the truth. "Thanks. I love that song."

"I figured you might."

"Why that one?"

Montee serenaded him with the first verse. Mitchell joined him for the rest of the song.

Montee squeezed him even tighter. "I was hoping that, wherever you were, you'd hear what was in my heart."

"I did."

They *looked* at each other. It was the type of look that could be followed by only one thing ...

Their first kiss was soft, slow, sweet, and *long*.

When their lips parted, they were both out of air.

"Damn," was all Montee could muster.

"That ... that was worth the eight-year wait," Mitchell admitted.

"Eight years, three months, and six days," Montee corrected.

They cracked up.

Montee leaned back against the driver's side of his car. He put his hands in his pockets. "So . . . here we are again."

"Yeah."

They stared in silence.

Mitchell finally broke it. "You have any other concert dates coming up?"

"I got a white pride event in San Diego next weekend."

"Ah. Who else is on the bill?"

"John Waters, Kate Clinton, and k.d. lang."

"So you're the solo Negro?"

"Yup. I usually am. But it don't bother me—being the solo Negro *pays*."

"I bet."

"And I make sure I'm in *every* picture taken. No one's gonna invite me to the party and expect me to stay in the background, like the help."

They laughed.

"I'll also be doin' Atlanta's Black Pride, Labor Day weekend. You should come down the week before. I can show you the city. We can hit a club and dance the night away. And you can hear my next CD before it hits stores in November."

"Sounds like fun. But I can't be away for a week."

"Yes, you can. Errol's gonna be hangin' with his boys and Destiny's gonna be hangin' with her grandparents. When's the last time you've been on a vacation?"

"A month before Destiny was born." He and Gene had gone to Honolulu for five days. It was a trip his mother paid for; as she put it, "This'll be the *only* vacation you take in the next eighteen years, so make sure you enjoy it."

"Uh-huh. And I bet you haven't even gone away for the *weekend* since she was born, huh?" Montee presumed.

"Uh . . . no."

"You know what they say: all work and no play. You can get rusty."

"Given the sounds emanating from you when I was bastin' that booty, I don't think so."

"Now, why you *even* . . ."

Mitchell giggled.

"Come on, you owe it to yourself to do somethin' *for* yourself. Just think about it, okay?" Montee wore that stray puppy-dog look again.

And, once again, Mitchell gave up. "Okay, I'll think about it."

"Jood."

Silence.

"Well . . . I gotta get to rehearsal."

"Have a jood rehearsal, and a jood show tonight."

"Thanks. I will. I had a better-than-*jood* time, again."

Mitchell smiled. "Me, too."

They embraced. After almost a minute, they let go. Mitchell planted a light kiss on his lips.

Montee grinned. "Thanks. You're paid in full. That was lick number fifty."

"That was one debt I was *very* happy to settle."

Montee opened his door and climbed in. He started the car and rolled down his window. "Ah, there's our so-long song."

They had met two years before Erykah Badu's debut came out. It took a moment to make the connection. Mitchell nodded. "Next lifetime."

"Next lifetime," Montee repeated.

"I think it's your turn to count off."

Montee held out his left hand; Mitchell took it. "One . . . two . . . two and a half . . ."

Mitchell chuckled.

Montee inhaled deeply. "Three."

Mitchell looked away as he took off up the block and turned the corner.

Mitchell had just made it back to the kitchen when the phone rang.

"Hello?"

"You answered on the first ring. You must be home-*alone*-osexual." It was Gene. He still knew *exactly* when to call. Some things never change.

"Yes, I am."

"So, in the immortal words of Sandra St. Victor, did he come over *and* over?"

"He did, but didn't."

"Huh?"

Mitchell filled him in on their evening and the morning after.

"All that slurpin', slappin', snackin', and smackin', and *no* shaggin'?" Gene cracked.

"There's more to life than shaggin'."

"Shaggin' is what life is all about. If it weren't, none of us would be here."

"That's not the kind of connection we made. Or have."

"Apparently."

"I guess we're only meant to . . . make you-know-what to each other with song. When we were singing together last night, and this morning . . . it was almost orgasmic."

"Well, I'm glad to hear it was *almost*. The last thing I needed was to be bailing you out of jail because you two violated some quality-of-life ordinance, spilling your juices in a public place—*and* in front of dozens of witnesses."

Mitchell chuckled. "He's invited me to Atlanta. I might go."

"*Might* go? Hmm . . . you only want him to be a friend with benefits."

How did he know? "Uh, yeah."

"Every home should have one, they always come in handy. But from what I saw, he'd want to be much more than that. No wonder you didn't go all the way: if you did, the celebrity would probably be stalking *you.*"

If he only knew that that shoe is on my foot . . . "Montee isn't the type to do that."

"Don't bet on it; the ones you don't think are capable of it are the ones who would boil a rabbit in a second. And speaking of bets: B.D. will be happy to hear he won ours."

"What bet?"

"He bet me and Babyface that you wouldn't go all the way with Montee. That child may be brain dense, but he is *very* perceptive."

Mitchell told B.D. about his first tryst with Montee—but not Gene or Babyface. And, eight years later, B.D. could also see that, no matter how right things felt with Montee, he was still the wrong man for Mitchell.

Mitchell was amused. "My best friends, gambling on my carnal conquests . . . ?"

"Ha, *some*body's got to."

"I'm appalled."

"You'll get over it. And you need to get over *it.*"

"Meaning?"

"*Meaning,* it's time you took a chance—or, rather, *the* chance."

To Mitchell's surprise, Gene has been pushing Mitchell to make *that* move. Gene was never pleased about Mitchell being in a relationship with Raheim; he didn't think the b-boy was jood enough for his best friend. But over time Raheim proved his devotion to Mitchell, impressing Gene. Given that Gene witnessed how broken up Mitchell was over their breakup and Raheim's addiction, one would assume that the very last thing he'd want to see them do is reunite (it's a total switch from

Gene's initial reaction to Mitchell and Raheim's love being on the rocks: he urged Mitchell to hire Marvin Mitchelson to sue for palimony).

Gene won't come out and say it, though; admitting it when he can't bring himself to even *say* the word *love* out loud would certainly bring on a seizure (the only person who has heard Gene speak it is Destiny, and they whisper it to each other as if it were a secret).

"It's time to snap out of that Stepford ex-wife mode," Gene continued. "You've spent entirely too much time obsessing over that house."

"I haven't been obsessed with it."

"Oh no? Last night at dinner you rhapsodized over finding a used cookie jar in the trash. *Hell-o?* If *that's* not obsessing, I don't know what is."

"You know I've been looking for it a long time," Mitchell countered.

"Yes, and I'm glad you found it. But now that you've added the finishing touch and the house is *done,* you will have to answer the same question that Mrs. Oliver Rose in *The War of the Roses* did: 'What's left to do?' "

Hmm…is that why my joy over finally finding it faded so fast?

"That house is the only thing you've had a serious relationship with in the past few years."

"That's not true."

"Yes, it is. And you know that Vinton doesn't count. He was truly you-know-who's understudy."

"I cared a lot about Vinton."

"I didn't say you didn't. But, it's obvious *why* you did. Imitations *do* come with limitations; as the Queen once wailed, 'Ain't *nothin*' like the real thing.' And, while I'm on that subject: What time *will* the real thing arrive this evening?"

"Six-thirty."

"*Jood.* Maybe you'll stop pining over that *nau*seatingly romantical clip of you two on Sodomite Sunday." The photo was taken on Gay Pride Day in the Village in 1993 and appeared in *The Baldwin Bulletin*, a Black SGL magazine; it shows Mitchell clutching Raheim by his bald head as they gaze into each other's eyes. It used to hang in the master bedroom; when they broke up, Mitchell retired it to a box at the very back of a closet he stored most of Raheim's belongings in. Mitchell hung it back up in his office after he ended his relationship with Vinton. "You're probably gushing over it right now," Gene assumed.

"I'm not in my office."

"For a *change*. It's time you started working on what can be—professionally *and* personally. And you don't have to worry about taking those steps by yourself. You won't be alone. I'll be right here."

Mitchell sighed. "I know."

"You two never said good-bye. And if good-bye really means *good-bye*, then so be it. You'll move on. And if it doesn't . . . in either case, you will *finally* stop waiting to exhale, so *I* can, too."

"You?"

"Yes, *me*. I feel like I've been holding *my* breath the past four years!"

Mitchell giggled. "I guess that's what a jood Judy is for, huh?"

"Indeed."

Raheim managed to get three washers and three dryers in their building's laundry room and finished in just under two hours. He was placing his father's folded clothes on his bed (including that jersey) when his cell rang.

He looked at the picture that popped up. He took a deep breath. It was Simon, his most recent ex. When they broke up, Simon said he would need some space before they could talk again. He said he'd call in six months; those six months were up.

They had met the Saturday immediately after Thanksgiving in 2001 at Gigi's, a restaurant in Times Square. Raheim and Angel were having a late lunch. Simon was their waiter. Actually, he wasn't, but asked the young lady whose station it was if he could serve them. And did he ever plan on serving them—or, rather, Raheim. Simon recognized Raheim as soon as he walked in: He had all three calendars released by All-American featuring Raheim, and ads ripped out of magazines and off telephone booths. He also had many of his commercials and almost every episode of *Smokin' Soundz*, the syndicated late-Friday-night music-video show Raheim hosted for two seasons on the WB, on tape. Simon just wasn't a fan—he was a fanatic.

And he had let Raheim know from the jump. "Hi, my name is Simon," he began, placing napkins and silverware before them, "and it will be *my* pleasure to serve you today, Mr. Rivers."

Angel chuckled to himself.

Raheim was taken aback; he hadn't been recognized in some time and it was obvious this man was interested. "Uh . . . thanks."

"Can I get you something to drink while you look over the menu?"

"Uh, just water for me," Raheim informed him.

"Are you sure? We have some great margaritas."

"Uh, no thanks."

Simon turned to Angel. "How about you, sir?"

"I'll have a Coke."

"Fine. I'll be back with your drinks." He winked at Raheim as he left.

Angel shook his head. "*Day-um*. Now, *that's* a junky trunk."

"That it is," agreed Raheim, his eyes following Simon's big bouncing buns.

"You better jump on that, yo."

"Man, I ain't even interested."

Angel wasn't buying it. "Since when you ain't interested in some a-z-z?"

"Since I got more important things to be concerned with."

"She-it, you ain't in recovery for a *sex* addiction. How long has it been?"

Raheim shrugged. "Like a year."

"*A year?* Man, you probably gonna explode any minute."

"I ain't goin' down that road right now. Gettin' involved with folks would be too complicated."

"You wouldn't say that if it was *Little Bit* grinnin' in yo' face."

Raheim cut his eyes. Angel knew *Little Bit* was a sore spot *and* a sore subject for him. It's bad enough Raheim lost Little Bit; he also had to swallow that Little Bit moved on with someone else. Angel told Raheim about spotting him and another brutha at Rockwell's in Brooklyn, all hugged up on the dance floor.

"You ain't gotta get involved," Angel maintained. "All you gotta do is get *in*. Nothin' says you can't have a little fun with your public. And even if you ain't into him, we can still milk this situation."

"We?"

"Well, you can, for the both of us. You could get us some free drinks, dessert, maybe even dinner on the house."

Raheim had used his celebrity status in restaurants before to his advantage but wasn't in the mood today. "I ain't playin' with this brutha like that."

"That's *exactly* what he wants ya to do."

Simon returned with their drinks. "I hope you don't mind, but I fixed you a cranberry-apple juice." He placed it in front of Raheim. "I think I read in *People* that it's your favorite. It's on the house."

Raheim was impressed; it *was* in *People*. "That was nice of you. Thanks."

"You're welcome. It's my pleasure."

"I bet it would be," Angel mumbled to himself.

"So, do you see anything on the menu you like, or would you like *me*"—both Raheim and Angel's eyebrows raised; they looked at each other, then Simon—"to recommend something?" Simon finished with a smile.

Since he hadn't gotten much play recently and did love the attention, Raheim decided to go along. "Since you know a little about my taste," he began, peeping Simon's ass, "why don't you pick a dish for me."

Simon's light brown eyes twinkled. "It will be my pleasure."

Simon chose the grilled chicken platter with roasted garlic potatoes and steamed broccoli, which Raheim loved. He also gave Raheim a complimentary slice of chocolate cake with a

scoop of vanilla ice cream (Angel settled on the pecan pie). Raheim left Simon a ten-dollar tip and Simon gave Raheim *three*
tips: his cell, home, and work numbers.

Raheim called the next day. The day after that, they went
out on their first date. And after that dinner and a movie
(*Training Day*), Simon invited Raheim to his apartment to see
the photos and posters he'd collected. Raheim stayed—and
played—the next two nights.

The sex was, as Raheim dubbed it, "off the mutha-fuckin'
chain-link fence." They twirled and tumbled and tackled in
every room, on every seat (including the toilet), in every nook
(like the walk-in closet). There was a ... *nicetyness* that de-
fined his encounters with Simon that didn't exist in any others, including Mitchell. He'd moan Mitchell's name in ecstasy;
Simon's, he'd *bark*. He'd beg Mitchell for mercy; with Simon,
he'd *sob* for it. He made sweet love with Mitchell; with Simon,
he made *freaky* love. Mitchell was the first man to turn him
out; Simon, the first to *churn* him out. And Raheim *needed*
this kind of release—he hadn't had any jood old-fashioned,
bangin'-the-headboard, soakin'-up-the-sheets, shoutin'-to-the-
heavens boot-knockin' in eons. The last few times he and
Mitchell were together Raheim had been going through the
motions, and the few hookups before Simon had been very
perfunctory (whip it out, strap it up, stick it in, grind it up,
jerk it out). With Simon it was always calculated and coordi-
nated yet very explosive. Sensual, yet seedy. Nice *and* nasty.

Because it wasn't a secret that Simon was infatuated with
Raheim the model, Raheim expected their lust affair to flame
out as soon as Simon grew tired of their conquests or got to
know Raheim the man.

But Simon surprised him. Even though Raheim spent the
night at his place three nights out of the week, Simon didn't
drop hints that he move in ("This is your side of the closet" or
"Here's a set of house keys"). Since Raheim was battling an

addiction, Simon attended Gam-Anon meetings, where the friends and family members of compulsive gamblers could discuss the part they could play in the recovery process. Simon helped Raheim study for his GED, which Raheim received last September. While he didn't know who Mitchell was, Simon heard through the grapevyne that Raheim had broken up with someone he'd been with for some time and that this man was helping to raise his son, as well as a daughter they adopted. Simon assured Raheim that he wouldn't interfere in the relationships Raheim had with his children, nor would he be insecure about or become jealous over his having contact with Mitchell. And he didn't pressure Raheim into making a commitment (although just about everything he did showed he hoped they were traveling in that direction).

Raheim also surprised himself. He didn't think he could feel anything for another man again after Mitchell, who was not only the first man he ever loved and fell in love with but his first love. Simon changed that; he was a *homie*-lover-friend. He wasn't gangsta, but put him in the right clothes or style and he'd fit the profile (Raheim found him even sexier with his Afro done in cornrows or wearing a 'do rag). They'd shoot hoops (the majority of the time Raheim won) and play handball (Simon was the usual champ). They'd ruffhouse, seeing who could throw, body-slam, and lock the other down (Simon often triumphed). They'd work out together; during one session, Raheim bet Simon he couldn't bench-press *him*—and he did. All of these activities became forms of foreplay: they'd work up a sweat and then get *really* sweaty.

Angel couldn't have been happier that his boyee was gettin' some—and gettin' it *jood*. Raheim's mother liked Simon and thought they made a cute couple ("If it ain't the Hershey's kiss and the Planters peanut"). And Raheim's father was also pleased his son was seeing someone—but curious about their "roles."

"You the man, right?" he asked, no doubt thrown by his son being with someone who was taller (three inches), more pumped up, and just as "manly" (his word) as Raheim (of course, the question had never arisen when Raheim was with Mitchell). Raheim didn't have the heart to tell him that, yes, his son regularly hollered "*You da man*" as he rode Simon like a mechanical bull or wrapped his thighs around Simon's neck as Simon dicked-him-the-fuck-down (ironically, his two favorite positions for Mitchell to bang him in), so he just said, "We both are." No doubt afraid of what *that* meant, Pop Rivers left that convo alone.

Raheim loved being with Simon, loved being around him, and *really* loved being inside of him and vice versa. And Raheim told Simon "I love you" and believed he did. But it became clear to Simon that he didn't (at least not in the way Simon hoped he did) last December when they happened to run into Mitchell and Destiny in Harlem. Raheim and Simon were coming from Raheim's mother's; Mitchell and Destiny were on their way to see Gene.

The scene was very reminiscent of Mitchell and Crystal's first meeting a decade before. While his father stood by paralyzed, Errol had to introduce his mother to Mitchell. This time, Destiny did the honors.

"Hi, my name is Destiny. What's yours?" she asked Simon, still in Raheim's arms.

"Simon."

"Ooh. Like the game, Simon Says?"

"Yes."

"Are you a friend of my uncle Raheim?"

"I am."

"Well, any friend of his is a friend of mine!"

They all laughed.

Destiny pointed to her father. "This is my daddy."

Her father put out his hand. "Mitchell."

Simon shook it. "Nice to meet you."

"You, too."

One wouldn't have known that since that was all they said to each other. Raheim and Destiny did the rest of the talking.

Simon said just as little after Raheim kissed Destiny and bid Mitchell good-bye. The reason why came out later that night.

"I saw the way you looked at him," Simon accused.

"What you talkin' about?"

"I *saw* the way you looked at him."

"What did you see? I wasn't lookin' at him any kind of way."

"You were."

"What way?"

Simon searched for the right words. "In a way I . . . I know you're never gonna look at me."

It was Raheim's turn to be silent. What could he say? He'd probably always known it was true. He loved Simon for all he did and how he made him feel, but didn't love *him*. And while he was in love with how Simon loved him, he wasn't in love with *him*. As Raheim learned, you can love the package but not the person occupying the package. Deep down, he wished it was Little Bit he was laughing with, taking these important steps with, sharing this new chapter in his life with. Maybe he'd hooked up with Simon to prove that he could move on like Little Bit had, but he hadn't moved on—he'd just moved Simon into Little Bit's place without recognizing that Simon had to create his own. And Raheim knew he hadn't been and wasn't in the space to let that happen.

Raheim had never seen Simon cry until that night. Simon refused to be comforted by him; he just wanted Raheim to leave. So he did.

Simon called the next day when he knew Raheim would be on a plane to Chicago to film a Pizza Hut commercial. His voice was shaky and solemn. "Hi. It's me. Um . . . I think . . . I . . . we can't be together anymore. I really love you but . . . this doesn't mean we won't speak again. I just need . . . time. I'll call you in like . . . six months. Uh . . . jood luck. I'll be thinking about you."

Raheim still has the message. Simon had always been a man of his word, but Raheim assumed this would be the last time he'd hear his voice—especially when, two weeks later, he received whatever belongings he left at Simon's, via parcel post. He could see him needing six days, even six weeks—but six *months*?

Raheim pressed the send button. "Hay."

"Hay Sweets."

Raheim still tingles when he refers to him as that. "It's jood to hear your voice, Boo Bear."

"Yours, too."

"How are you?"

"I could be better. But I'm here. You?"

"Uh . . . I'm jood."

"Jood. I'm glad."

"I wish *you* were feelin' jood."

"Me, too. But I will again soon. At least I don't feel like I did months ago."

"Uh . . . I . . . I wanted to call, but . . ."

"It's a jood thing you didn't. If I heard your voice I wouldn't have been nice. I had . . . a lot inside. And I had to deal with it. Making you feel bad might've made me feel better, but it wouldn't help me get better."

Raheim decided to change the subject altogether. "Thanks for my gift." Simon had sent him an aqua-blue French Connection shirt.

"You're welcome. Happy belated."

"Thanks."

"What did you do?"

"Pop cooked dinner for me, and made me a cake."

"Nice. You've got a fifteen-year-old son. You're really gettin' up there." Simon snickered.

"You ain't too far behind me." He'll be twenty-eight next month. "What do you plan to do for yours?"

"I don't know. Milt is talkin' about headin' to New Orleans." Milt, or Milton, is Simon's best friend. He reminds Raheim of Gene, the mouth that roared. It seems almost every friend has a best friend like them.

"How is Milt?"

"He's jood. We'll be working the seven o'clock to L.A. tomorrow night." They're both flight attendants with United. They were put on six-month furloughs after the 9/11 attacks. When Simon was called back in April last year, Raheim always arranged to fly with him (having someone he knew on board made him less jittery) and Simon knew how to take care of him—he made sure Raheim got as much food as he wanted and never deplaned without a bottle of bubbly or sparkly (which they'd share at Raheim's hotel room). And because of Simon's careful planning, Raheim had flown first class on companion passes with him to Paris, Santo Domingo, and Bangkok. In January, Raheim switched his preferred carrier to Continental so they wouldn't run into each other.

"I miss serving you," Simon disclosed.

"I miss that, too. Nobody can serve me in the air *or* on the ground like you."

Raheim could see and feel Simon blush.

Raheim wasn't sure if he should say it but did anyway. "And, I miss *you*."

Simon's blush turned into a smile. "I miss you, too."

"I'm sorry."

"For what?"

"For . . . for everything."

"You shouldn't be. Everything was jood between us."

"I mean, I . . . I didn't mean to hurt you."

"Now, usually when a man says that, he don't mean it. But I

know you do. And you really didn't hurt me. You never made promises that we'd be together; you never made *any* promises. You gave what you could and it was more than enough. It was probably too much: I fell in love with you." He sighed. "That's what happens when I fall for a fantasy."

"So, I was just a fantasy to you?"

"You were until the day you walked into the restaurant!"

They laughed.

"Uh . . . do you regret us meeting that day?" Raheim hesitantly asked.

"No. I regret getting in over my heart. Milton told me to be careful. He said you were probably on the boomerang."

"On the boomerang?"

"Yeah. He said when you love someone hard, it's *hard* to get over. There's so much history and your lives are still so connected, so interconnected. And because there is so much unfinished business, chances are you'll probably boomerang back to them."

"I haven't boomeranged back."

"*Yet*," Simon bluntly stated. He huffed. "Ya know, in a way, I *do* regret meeting you when I did."

"Why?"

"Because, if it had been years earlier, someone else would've been the stand-in and *I'd* be the one you'd be boomerangin' back to."

"I . . . I wish things coulda be different."

"Me, too."

"I do love you."

"I know you do. I felt it. I still feel it."

"And, this is gonna sound like a cliché but . . . I'd like to be friends."

"You're right, it *is* a cliché. I think we can be but . . . not right now."

"I understand."

Silence.

Simon sighed. "Every time I bench press two twenty-five, I'll be thinkin' of you."

Raheim giggled. "I hope that's a jood thing."

"It is."

S o, what did the letter say?" Mitchell asked as he finished retwisting Errol's hair.

That morning, Errol had received something from Yale, one of the many Ivy Leagues courting him. He's a hot commodity on the higher-education market: a Black male with a 3.97 GPA and a combined SAT score of 1520, who isn't an athlete *first*. And his being such an overachiever at such a young age (he skipped the third and sixth grades) will make him a Major Catch for the college that manages to sign him up.

The letter from Yale was probably yet another gauntlet thrown down in the war to woo him. At the moment, Yale, Stanford, Princeton, and MIT are tops on his list; he'll be visiting each campus this summer.

Errol slightly tilted his head back. "I didn't open it yet." He was parked on the floor, between Mitchell's legs. Mitchell was on the sofa. They were in the parlor.

"Why not?"

"I . . . I don't wanna deal with it until the weekend is over."

"Okay."

Silence.

"I was thinking . . . maybe I should just go to Columbia."

Hmm . . . it's not even on his B-list. "Why?"

"It's a jood school—as you know."

"Yes, I do." Mitchell graduated from Columbia's Journalism School in 1990. But the university didn't offer the type of aeronautic/astronautic program Errol was interested in. Mitchell recalled having a similar exchange with him a few weeks before, about NYU. "Are you still having butterflies about leaving home?"

"Nah," he immediately shot back. "I . . . I just want to make sure I'm covering all the bases."

"Don't worry. You are."

Silence.

"Sure you and Destiny will be all right without me?"

"Destiny won't. But I'll be fine once I turn that room of yours into my den."

Errol nudged him in the left thigh with his arm. "Funny."

"And, since I brought that up: Have you cleared that path yet?"

"Yes. Dad will be able to see the floor in my room. He'll be able to *eat* off of it, if he wants."

Mitchell had thought he'd heard the vacuum cleaner while he was doing laundry in the basement. Errol had never Hooverized his own floor before. Mitchell knew that only his father's homecoming could prompt Errol to turn into Felix Unger.

"I just hope he doesn't look in your closet . . ." Mitchell figured that was where Errol had probably put everything that was on the floor.

"I hope so, too." Errol snickered.

Mitchell checked out his work. "There. All done."

Errol popped up and headed for the mirror in the half bath. Mitchell couldn't see him but he knew what he was doing: tossing his head from side to side. And he also knew what he'd say.

"Lookin' *real* jood. Thanks."

Mitchell ducked his head inside. "You're welcome. Your hair

will be as long as Destiny's soon. Make sure you wrap it up tonight before you go to bed."

"I will."

The doorbell rang.

"I'll get it," Errol volunteered.

It was Crystal. She was dropping off a bag of presents and the two pies (both cherry) she'd made for the party. Errol was more interested in the dessert. After hugging and kissing her, he grabbed them. He took a long whiff of the aroma. "Mmm. My favorite. Thanks, Mom."

"You're welcome." As Errol walked up the hallway, she embraced Mitchell. "How are you today?"

"I'm jood."

"Oh?" She recognized there was something different about that "jood." She stepped back, looking at him quizzically. "What's his name?"

"Huh?"

"You've been with a man, haven't you?" she declared in her best Sophia Petrillo tone.

Mitchell glanced back in Errol's direction. "Crystal . . ."

"If I know my son, he's already slicing into one of those pies, so he is paying us dust."

Mitchell closed and locked the door. "How do you know?"

"A woman *knows* these things. I'm glad one of us is gettin' some."

"Your husband still holding out?" She had confided in Mitchell about Winston, whose interest in intimacy went from a frenzy in their fourth year of marriage to a funk in their fifth (and current) one.

"Yes. But now, instead of once a month, it's once every two weeks."

"At least he's doubled the dose."

"I'll throw him a ticker-tape parade when he quadruples it."

"Well, I didn't get some, but I did get some*thing*."

She looped her arm in his. "Believe me, *some*thing is better than *no*thing." They both laughed, heading for the kitchen.

Some would call their relationship strange. Bizarre. Even unreal. After all, there probably aren't many heterosexual women who, upon learning that the father of her child is not heterosexual, would allow his significant male other to continue to play a role in that child's life.

But Crystal isn't your (stereo)typical Baby Mama and theirs isn't your (stereo)typical Baby Mama Drama Tale.

After Crystal became Mrs. Winston Sledge in June 1997, Mitchell felt it was time for Raheim to tell her the truth about himself—and them. Of course, he balked. But Mitchell pressed him, arguing that now was as jood (and, in some respects, safe) a time as any. She didn't react the way Raheim thought; she didn't cry, curse, or carry on. Yes, she was upset, hurt, angry, even confused. But it wasn't because she felt jilted or rejected because Raheim was now with a man; she had moved on and found a man of her own who made her very happy.

And it wasn't because Raheim introduced Mitchell into their son's life and presented him as one thing when he was something else. Would she have agreed to let her son have an openly gay man for a godfather? She admitted she probably wouldn't have (even though her son's father wasn't straight). But she was a very different person back then and would not have given him the chance to prove that he was worthy. Whatever concerns or fears she might have had had already been erased by the time the truth was out.

It was about Raheim. He was, at least on the surface, bisexual—if not in his orientation at least in his expression. Even if he wasn't gay all the way he was gay *half* the way, and even she knew that didn't happen overnight. He'd known all along; he *had* to. And that was the kicker: he had not only been able to fool her, he'd also made a fool *of* her. It wasn't about whether he wasn't man enough or she was too much woman (which is what too many women ignorantly and arrogantly reduce these situations to). It was about playing with her emotions, playing with her heart, playing with her love. And not only did he play with her, he *played* her by bringing the person who, in at least a figurative sense, was standing in the way of her family really being a family. No matter what Raheim said, no matter what he did over the years, she had faith that they would one day be a them again. And even though she had a husband, a new family of her own, there was still a tiny part of her that felt Mitchell had taken *her* place. And was helping to raise *her* son. With *her* baby's daddy. The man she wanted to be *her* husband.

If Mitchell had been in her shoes, he would've blown a gasket, too.

She felt betrayed. Deceived. Used. The love, the life they shared, had been a masquerade. An act. A lie. And if she felt she could not trust the father of her son, a man she thought she knew for a decade, how could she trust his . . . his . . . *friend* with her son?

But she got over the shock, and then shocked Mitchell when, just a month after getting the news, called and requested to talk with him in person. He hadn't expected to hear from her—especially since, according to Raheim, she promised that "He will never see *my* son again." Mitchell knew that that might be the price he had to pay but just prayed she would come around sooner rather than later.

They met at a coffee shop not far from where she worked on a rainy Saturday afternoon. It's a meeting that Raheim was not (and, as far as she knows, still isn't) privy to. She didn't want to know all the details of their "affair" (as she labeled it)—where they met, when it began, when they started seeing each other exclusively. She wanted to talk about the person who would be most affected by the revelation and its aftermath: Junior.

"I see how jood you are with him," she observed. "I see how much he enjoys being with you. And . . . I know he doesn't want that to stop."

"It doesn't have to."

"No. It doesn't." She sighed heavily. "I'm . . . I'm just having a hard time digesting everything. And I guess I don't feel . . ."

"Safe?"

"Yeah."

"I can't say I know how you feel. But I don't feel safe right now either."

"Why?"

"I . . . I'm afraid of losing them. It was the hardest thing in the world for Raheim to tell you and Junior. We knew that it wouldn't be easy on anyone and that there was a chance . . . things might not be the same again. Telling you both could send Raheim over the edge; he's trying to hold it together, but I know he's on shaky ground. And Junior . . ." He took a deep breath. "I know what it's like to have the world you thought you lived in suddenly change overnight and not know what to do, to not know what your place in it is."

She considered what he said. "To keep it a secret this long . . . it must have been hard on you."

"I hated *being* the secret. Or, rather, the *open* secret. I always felt that you . . . might have been suspicious. That you . . . knew."

"Uh . . . I wouldn't say that I *knew* knew. But I knew something was . . . up. He didn't have any other girlfriends—or at least he didn't bring any around me and Junior. That alone didn't mean much; I dated a few men but never brought them around him or Junior. But he did bring *you* around. I saw the way Junior interacted with you—and the way Raheim was trying *not* to interact with you. One day my mother asked, 'Do you think they could be?' And I said, 'They could be what?' And she said, '*You* know what.' I told her no, but I had thought it before.

I guess I didn't want to recognize that it might be so. That she had seen it, too, and verbalized it . . . hearing about it out loud scared me. So I just ignored it. So long as *I* didn't speak it, it wasn't and couldn't be so."

"Raheim decided to be blind to it, too. Thinking no one could see how he felt for me."

"I . . . I don't want to hate him. Or you. I suppose it would be easy to do. It would also be very convenient and a waste of time. The fact is, I don't want any of us to suffer—not even Raheim, no matter how mad I am at him right now." She sighed heavily again. "I guess that's what we get."

He stared at her, puzzled.

"Falling in love with the same man."

He acknowledged that with a nod.

"And, we've both had our hearts broken by him."

His eyes widened.

"Lucky guess." She shrugged.

A very jood guess.

"And . . . we both love his son."

He placed his hand on hers. It meant so much to hear her say that. She smiled; Mitchell was reminded of why Raheim had nicknamed her Sunshine.

"Junior knows that I . . . well, I am *uncomfortable*, as he put it, with everything. But no matter how uncomfortable I may be, the last thing I want him to do is be uncomfortable and think that whatever is going on between his mommy and daddy is his fault. So . . . could you help?"

"What do you want me to do?"

"Just continue doing what you've been doing. I'm still working out my feelings. Some things I'm not sure of. But one thing I am sure of is your devotion to him. And there's no reason why he shouldn't continue to receive that devotion, especially at a time when things are so . . . unstable."

He caressed her hand. "However I can be there, I will be."

"Thanks."

"You don't have to thank me; it's a blessing, being there for him, for all of you. And, he may not be able to see it right now, but Raheim is very lucky that you are the mother of his son."

She rolled her eyes. "Raheim is lucky he has *us* to put up with him."

They laughed. And then they spent the next two hours comparing notes about the man they'd both fallen in love with—and the little boy they both loved.

They made a pact that day to do all they could to ensure that Junior felt safe—even if they didn't.

That she was able to face and come to terms with all of this was a testament to her maturity (not to mention jood common sense). The resentment toward Raheim didn't disappear overnight; that took a few years. She didn't, though, direct any of it toward Mitchell. While Mitchell thought Mrs. Rivers, Raheim's mother, was the cheerleader most responsible for Crystal's turnaround (upon being told by her son that he and Mitchell were a couple, she exclaimed, "Tell me something I *don't* know!" and immediately called Mitchell to express her pleasure in having a "son-in-law" like him), someone else indirectly influenced her handling this situation with such a level head: Raheim's father. Mr. Rivers had abandoned Raheim and his mother when Raheim was five, and Raheim was still dealing with the residual effects of that. Crystal realized that keeping Mitchell away from Junior when his development had been positively impacted by Mitchell's presence for half his life could seriously jeopardize his current (and future) mental and emotional health. She didn't want Junior to be torn up and conflicted as Raheim had been, filled with so much angst and anger. And she wasn't about to be one of those bitter mothers

who puts her own ambivalent feelings, selfish needs, or misguided beliefs ahead of her child's well-being.

So things stayed the same; the only thing that changed was
the guise under which they all interacted. Mitchell was no
longer just Junior's godfather but Raheim's "mate," as Crystal
dubbed him (Mitchell rejected the outdated "lover," and
"boyfriend" was a bit too juvenile for him and a bit too close for
comfort for Crystal since that's what Raheim once was to her).
Even though Junior now had a stepfather, Mitchell attended
those "father and son" events with Junior when Raheim's dis-
appearing acts began. When Mitchell and Raheim split, the
breakup didn't break up the relationship Mitchell had with Junior or the one he was cultivating with Crystal. When Junior
was accepted into Brooklyn Tech in the spring of 2000, there
was no question as to (nor was there a formal discussion about)
whom he would live with to attend the high school. And when
Errol began attending classes at Tech, Raheim started splitting
the eight-hundred-fifty-dollar child support payment with
Crystal; each month, they both sent Mitchell a check.

Thanks to their collective efforts, Errol is a well-rounded,
well-*grounded* young man, who has made them all proud.
That's not to say he's been a complete angel. There have been
some bumps in the road, and most of them have come during
the teen years. But compared to the tribulations other teens put
their parents through, even his major infractions have been
somewhat minor. He's talked back, neglected to do his chores,
and broken curfew. Last year, he skipped school to go to the first
showing of *The Scorpion King* (that got him grounded for a
week). Four months ago, he, Monroe, and Sidney decided to
take Monroe's father's car for a joyride (never mind that none
of them has a license *or* a permit). They didn't get far; they
backed into a fire hydrant trying to get out of the parking space
(that earned Errol a month on lockdown and the allowance he

would have received over two months went to help pay for the damage done to the car).

And then there's this past Thursday, his birthday, when he came home with his left ear pierced. Mitchell knew Crystal would have something to say about that. She inspected it as Mitchell had done days earlier—and wore the same frown he had. "And why did you do it?" She even asked the same first question.

He gave her the same answer. "Because it looks jood."

"Uh-huh. Well, it *does* look jood. But I'd appreciate it if, for the next three years, you'd consult us before putting any other holes in your body—or designs *on* your body."

Errol wore that busted look. "How you know?"

"A mother knows."

Mitchell giggled to himself.

"So, is it in an area you wouldn't be embarrassed to show me?" she queried.

He lifted his T-shirt on his right side. A couple of inches above his waist was a heart with an arrow through it and "Mom" was spelled out in the center.

She grinned. "I guess I can't argue with that, huh? You plan to get any other work done?"

"I might get another tattoo. And I might get my right ear done."

"Hmmph. *I might* for you means *I will.* I just don't want you walking around looking like you just got out of—or belong in—prison."

"Okay. I won't be. Uh, how long you staying?"

"Are you tryin' to get rid of me already?"

"I'm just asking."

"Uh-huh. Don't worry, I won't be here when your homies start to arrive. Couldn't give them the impression you're a mama's boy, now, could we?"

His cell phone rang (he's under Mitchell's family and friends plan). He took it off his belt clip and looked at the name and number. "May I be excused?"

Crystal clutched her chest with both hands. "So, you'd rather talk to one of those little hoochies than visit with your mama?"

"I won't be long," he argued. "She . . . needs directions."

Mitchell and Crystal glanced at each other. "Sure she does," they echoed together.

She waved him on. "Go ahead."

He kissed her on the cheek. "Thanks, Mom." He answered it. "Hay." He jogged out of the kitchen.

"How did you know about the tattoo?" Mitchell asked.

"He had mentioned it a while back, saying he might want to do it and get his ear pierced on his birthday. He was just throwing them both out there to see what I would say."

"And what did you say?"

"Nothing. I knew he wanted to and I didn't have a problem with him doing either one. At least he picked something sane." She looked around. "You sure I can't help you with anything?"

"No. Thanks for offering. Would you like a cup of coffee?"

"Sure. Thanks."

He poured one for them both. They sat down. They sipped.

She huffed. "Now, tell me the truth . . ." She clutched her cheeks and turned her head to the left, in profile. "Do I look *old* enough to have a fifteen-year-old son?"

"No, you don't."

"It seems it was just yesterday that I was bringing him home from the hospital. Now he's a young stud. God, I sound like one of those irritating mothers in those cheesy movies they show on *Lifetime*."

Mitchell giggled.

"Oh, before I forget." She went into her pocketbook and pulled out a purple envelope. "It's from my mother."

"What is it?"

"I don't know. Open it and we'll find out."

Printed on the front of the card in Monaco-style lettering was:

HAPPY FATHER'S DAY TO A SPECIAL MAN.

Mitchell was *stunned*—and not just because Father's Day was *next* Sunday. "*Your* mother gave this to me?"

"Yup."

That her mother would send him a card of *any* kind was a shock in and of itself. While others might have felt the same way, she was the only member on Crystal's side of the family to vocalize her horror over her only grandson being in the company of "one of those people" (as she argued, since Raheim wasn't gay all the way, there was hope for him—and only a fifty-fifty chance Errol would turn out "like that"). When Crystal wouldn't cut ties with Mitchell, her mother refused to acknowledge him at family gatherings—and if there was a family gathering at her apartment, wouldn't invite him. They'd never even had a conversation; before the truth came out, their contact was minimal and their exchanges usually consisted of "Hello" and "How are you?" So receiving a gift from her— especially one like this—was a big deal.

He opened it:

One day just isn't enough
To truly celebrate all you are and do
So here's a reminder that you're thought of
Not just today but the whole year through!
Enjoy Your Day
Georgia

The sentiment was very short, very simple, but very sweet. And Mitchell was . . . well, *stunned* by it. "*Wow.*" He handed it to Crystal.

She read it and was stunned, too. "Well, *I'm* jealous. I didn't even get a Mother's Day card from her!"

"How nice. I'll have to thank her."

"I'll call you when I'm with her tonight and put her on the phone. I can't wait to see her face." She nudged him with her elbow. "Looks like you've finally converted her . . ."

". . . figuratively speaking," he finished with her.

They laughed. The house phone rang. Mitchell answered it. "Hello?"

"Hay," Raheim said. He can't say "Little Bit" anymore but doesn't like calling Mitchell by his name. So he doesn't call him anything.

"Hey. How are you?"

"I'm jood. You?"

"I'm jood, too."

Silence.

"I just wanted to know, what time I should come over?" Raheim already knew what time to come over. It may sound silly, but he just wanted to hear his voice. He missed hearing his jood friend's voice every day like he used to.

"Around six-thirty."

"Should I bring somethin'?" Raheim also knew the answer to that, too.

"I don't think so. I think we've got everything taken care of."

"A'ight. I'll see you then."

"Okay."

Silence again.

Finally Raheim says what he doesn't want to say. "Bye."

"Bye."

Raheim hesitates before hanging up—and notices, for the first time, he's not the only one.

If you want *the* best chicken in Harlem—be it baked, barbecued, broiled, grilled, smoked, roasted, smothered, or fried—the Chicken Kitchen is the place to go. It actually looks like a chicken shack—the sloppy plywood decor is what Grace, Raheim's mother, was going for when she decided to open up a restaurant. She wanted the place to have a way down-home feel, like folks were stepping into a juke joint. But the CK, as many of the teens and twentysomethings call it on the streets, is not the least bit seedy. In fact, it's become the family hangout on weekends (a stream of baby strollers will be parked outside the place) and a prime stop on many bus tours through Harlem.

It has achieved this status in less than three years, and no one is more surprised by its success than its owner. In late 1999, Grace had put in her twenty years working for the city and was all too ready to leave (she was offered an early retirement package that was too jood to pass up). But she got bored quick—in a week. At forty-nine, she didn't want to spend the rest of her life *watching* the rest of her life pass her by in some retirement village in Florida, and she was years away from buying and settling into her dream home in Greenville, North Carolina (where her family is from). So she volunteered at the local Red

Cross and Boys and Girls Club, but neither was very fulfilling (they were more stressful than the job she left).

Her grandson provided her with the answer during a weekend visit. He was chowing down on her famous barbecue chicken when . . .

"Grandma, you should open up a restaurant."

"Me? Open a restaurant?"

"Yes. Why not?"

"I don't know the first or last thing about runnin' a business."

"You can learn."

"And the *last* thing Harlem needs is another soul-food restaurant."

"Then don't open a soul-food restaurant."

"What kind of restaurant, then?"

"Do the specialty thing."

"The specialty thing?"

"Yes. I learned about that in marketing class. You can concentrate on one type of food—like chicken—and serve it up in a variety of ways. You got so many jood recipes."

The more she thought about it, the more she thought . . . why not? Not only would it give her something to do, that something would be something she loved to do and she might even make a little money doing it. And even if it didn't fly, at least she couldn't say she didn't try. So, she took an adult-education class at Hunter College on starting your own business; pooled her own resources (fifteen thousand dollars of the equity she had in the co-op Raheim purchased for her in '95) with grants from minority and women's business initiatives throughout the city; chose a lot on Adam Clayton Powell Jr. Boulevard (two blocks south of 125th Street, close enough to but away from the maddening crowds); and, three months after signing a lease, had her grand opening on her birthday: New Year's Day 2001.

Since her grandson had come up with the idea, she let him

name the place. He didn't have to think longer than ten seconds. "The Chicken Kitchen."

"The Chicken Kitchen," she repeated. "I *love* it."

And so do Lou Rawls, Al Green, Eddie and Gerald Levert, B.B. King, James Brown, Shirley Caesar, Russell Simmons, LL Cool J, and Magic Johnson; they all stopped by, sampled the grub, and took photos with her. Even white public figures such as Mayor Mike Bloomberg and former President Bill Clinton have visited (they were running for office or opening *up* an office in the community). The number one celeb, though, is and has always been her son—snapshots of him as an A-A model, holding his Independent Spirit Award moments after winning, and standing by her side on opening day remain in the very center of her wall of fame. Raheim is almost never recognized, though—and he likes it that way. As far as he is concerned, his mom is the true star; along with Eva Isaac, the Queen of the Apollo Theater, she's become another Mother of Harlem. And with Harlem looking like the Mall of America thanks to Ben & Jerry's, HMV, and the Disney Store on 125th Street, the restaurant has become a community center, a home away from home for folks to not only eat but meet and greet.

When Raheim entered, she was greeting new customers and catching up with the regulars. Like Sylvia of Sylvia's, she wants them to know there is a real person behind the name (even if the restaurant isn't named after her).

She smiled as he approached. "Oh, excuse me," she told a young man and woman seated at one of the six fountain tables in the restaurant. "Thanks again for your business and please come again."

"Hay, Ma." He bear-hugged her.

"Hi, honey."

"How are you?"

"I'm quite jood. And you?"

"Ditto."

"You wanna eat somethin'?"

"I'm not hungry."

"Since when has that ever stopped you?"

"Uh, I guess I can have a little somethin'."

"Okay. You want the usual?"

"Yeah."

His usual is the most popular item on the menu: the chicken pot pie, which has carrots, peas, corn, green beans, potatoes, chunks of white meat, and Grace's Groovy Gravy. Food critics from as far away as D.C., Chicago, and L.A. have raved about it and entire sports teams (from junior high-schoolers to pro ballers) have made special trips to buy one (some will approach the counter and ask for "the 3Gs"). This has caught the attention of General Mills: they're interested in packaging and selling the dish in supermarkets across the country. They've been in discussions to purchase the rights for two months.

They sat in her eating nook, a small room next to her office. She watched as he dug into his first pie (he usually eats three). "They came with another offer," she revealed.

"And?"

"I said no."

"You tryin' to break their bank?"

"No. It's not about the money; it's about havin' a say. We don't need a contract for them to just steal the recipe and run, and that's what they'd be doin' if I signed."

"They must really want it if they came back twice."

"Well, that's the problem: they want *it*, they don't want *me*, and we are a team. You can't have one without the other. They're supposed to be sending some VP down here next week to talk to me."

"Uh-huh, to talk some sense *into* you."

She nodded. "That's what Rico said. But it won't matter. She'll be wasting her time and mine."

"How is Rico?" Rico is Enrico, her boyfriend from the Dominican Republic. He's a forty-seven-year-old divorced father of two she's been dating exclusively for about two years. They met at one of the quarterly mixers thrown by the city for small-business owners of color (he owns two restaurants, both called Enrico's, in the Bronx). Raheim is happy about the relationship since he hasn't seen her with anyone in twenty-five years (that last and only person being his father). They're sort of an odd couple: he's three inches shorter than she (the height difference doesn't bother her; as she confided, "He's got the inches where it *really* counts").

"He's jood. He should be stopping by with his grandkids in about an hour."

"All of them?"

"Yup, all of them."

"Mmm . . ."

"Mmm, what?"

"Nothin'."

"That *mmm* wasn't nothin'."

"They comin' to meet their future grandma."

"I don't think so."

"Come on, Ma: Why else would he be bringin' the whole posse?"

"To eat?"

"Uh-huh. How old are they again?"

"Nine, eight, six, five, three, and two."

"That's a Brady bunch."

"I know. Tomorrow is Maya's birthday; she's the youngest. I made a cake for her, too."

"See, you bakin' birthday cakes for *all* your grandkids."

She pinched him on his right arm. "Unless you have other plans, I'll continue to be the grandmother of *one*." Rico has been hinting they should marry, but she's avoided even talking about it; she's not interested in becoming a Mrs. again.

As he started on his second pie, she placed her elbows on the table, leaning forward. "So . . . are you ready to go *home?*"

"Huh?"

"You heard. You haven't been *home* in some time."

"I was there last Sunday." He'd taken Errol back to Brooklyn after his weekend visit with his mother.

"Well, dropping off your son is different from being invited inside."

That it is. He remembers the last time he was inside—April 16, 1999. The night before, he was supposed to attend a dinner to celebrate Mitchell's thirty-third birthday, hosted by Babyface, B.D., and Gene. He didn't show up, and when he showed up at the house later that eve, he looked through the window to see Mitchell on the sofa, crying. Destiny was lying against his side, asleep. The image was a moment of cruel déjà vu: his mother in that same spot on their sofa, sobbing over his father's unannounced exit, as he consoled her. After Mitchell left early that morning, Raheim crept inside and left him a note that simply said: "I'm sorry." He couldn't bear to face him. While Mitchell has never said he wasn't welcome since that night, Raheim hasn't felt . . . *worthy*.

Raheim did attempt to deflect some of the blame for their relationship ending, complaining to his mother that when Destiny came along Mitchell forgot all about him and that's why he turned to gambling. She was just as upset as he was that it was over between them, so he believed he'd get a much-needed pat on the back—but received a slap across the face instead. As he was recovering from the shock (she had never hit him before), she apologized for striking him but broke it down like only a mother could . . .

You sure you ain't been sniffin' or smokin' or shootin' up somethin', too? He didn't drop you when Destiny came along; you chose to drop out when she did. Don't be angry with him because he had the jood sense to do what had to be done. Did you expect him to put his life and his daughter's life on hold for you? You oughta be thankin' him: he's the one who has been tryin' to hold everything together. Despite what you've done and put him through, he's been there for you and he still loves you—and love ain't the reason he should stay with you, it's the reason he shouldn't. And if you forget that, remember who you chose to be your son's godfather. Don't forget who stepped in to care for and be there for him when you stepped out . . .

Needless to say, he was slapped back into reality.

He has faced and accepted another reality: Mitchell, Errol, and now Destiny will decide whether he can visit again—permanently. He couldn't handle that kind of test a year ago, a month ago, not even a week ago.

But today? "Ain't no big deal."

His mother wasn't convinced. "Ah. It is always wise to put up a brave front."

"Ma, it ain't no big deal."

"We're talking about your son, your goddaughter, and the love of your life. It is a *very* big deal."

"I'm goin' to help my son celebrate his birthday."

"Mmm-hmm."

"And help Li—"

Her eyebrows raised.

"Help Mitchell cohost."

"*Uh-huh,*" she purred like Jackee Harry. "Just remember that you're stepping into a whole new world tonight—and I don't mean the kind Peabo and Regina were singin' about."

"Ma, I'm gonna be a'ight. Don't worry."

"How can I not? That's what mothers do."

"Thanks for bein' concerned. If anybody has to worry, it's me. I made this bed; now I gotta lie in it."

"Uh-huh. And you want *Little Bit* in it with you."

He nearly choked on his food. "Ma!"

She giggled.

Raheim held the cake in the palm of his left hand. "Maybe I should stick around and meet my future stepnieces and nephews."

"Get out of here." She walked him to the entrance. "Now, have a jood time."

"I will."

"And give my grandson a hug and kiss for me."

"I will."

"I would tell you to give Mitchell a hug and kiss from me, but I don't wanna be stirrin' up stuff—*yet*."

He giggled.

"Give *Destiny* the hug and kiss. Give *him* my best."

"I will."

"And give *me* a hug and kiss."

He did.

"Love ya, Ma."

"Love you, too, baby."

Mr. Rivers?"

Raheim was about to open the brownstone's front gate. He turned. "Yes?"

"I'm Sidney. Sid for short."

"And I'm Monroe. Everybody calls me Roe."

Raheim shook both their hands. "It's jood to meet you two. I've heard a lot about you both."

"Well, I hope you won't hold what you heard about him against me." Sidney chuckled.

Monroe frowned. "Not funny."

"I saw you on *Special Victims Unit* last week," Sidney continued. "You were jood."

Raheim smiled; his hallmark word was being passed on to another generation. "Thanks."

Sidney piped in. "I missed you on TV. But me and my pops saw you on the train platform down at Wall Street a couple of weeks ago."

"The Brooks Brothers ad on the 4/5 line?" The entire station is wall-to-wall BB—and, yeah, he's the only colored man out of the two dozen models featured.

"Yeah. Uh, did they let you keep the suit?"

"Man!" Sidney groaned.

Monroe shrugged, clueless. "What?"

Raheim chuckled under his breath. "You two came without dates?"

"My girlfriend is comin' with her best friend," explained Sidney.

"And my girl*friends* will start arrivin' in a half hour." Monroe grinned.

Sidney cut his eyes. "So he thinks."

Raheim motioned for them to go in first. "Let's get out of this rain."

Monroe rang the bell. Mitchell opened the door.

"Hay Mr. C," Sidney and Monroe harmonized.

"Evenin' gents. You two look jood."

"Thanks," they echoed.

"Where's E?" Monroe asked.

"Upstairs, still gettin' ready."

Monroe headed for the stairs. "He was gettin' ready when I called him a hour ago."

"Man, you should talk," snapped Sidney. "You spent a half hour in the bathroom shavin' them two hairs on your chin." He turned to Mitchell and Raheim. "Excuse us." He dropped his umbrella in a stand near the door and followed Monroe.

Mitchell smiled at Raheim. "Hey."

"Hay."

"Come on in." Mitchell closed the door behind him.

Raheim inhaled deeply. He felt . . . *at home*. Like he never left.

"Let me take your hat and jacket."

Raheim took them off; Mitchell hung them up on the hooks Raheim had mounted to the back of the door years ago.

Mitchell eyed the box Raheim had placed on the hall bureau. "Is that the cake?"

"Yeah." Raheim picked it back up. "Where do you want it to go?"

"In the fridge for now."

Raheim followed him into the kitchen. Mitchell opened the refrigerator. "You can place it right there." Raheim did. "Would you like something to drink?"

"Sure."

"We have orange juice, orange-pineapple juice, grape juice, cranberry juice, apple juice . . ." He looked up. "This is a juice house."

"So I hear."

"Maybe you'd like a cran-apple mix?"

He remembered . . . "That sounds jood."

As Mitchell made his drink, they were silent.

Raheim took his drink. "Thanks."

"You're welcome. Please, have a seat."

They both did, across from each other, at the island.

"So you finally met the other Musketeers."

"Yeah."

"They remind me."

Raheim knew who they reminded him of . . .

"Speaking of: Have you seen Angel lately?"

"We hung out last night."

"Ah. How is he?"

"He's jood."

"Jood."

Raheim sipped. "My moms sends you her best."

"Do send her mine. How is she?"

"She's jood."

"Jood."

"Where's Destiny?"

"She's at my mother's for the weekend. Oh, before I forget . . ." Mitchell went into the dining area and took something off the table. He returned. "This is for you."

The standard-size piece of construction paper was powder blue. Outlined in glued rainbow glitter was a giant cake with a

single lighted candle. Written in green Crayola in the body of
the cake was the message:

Uncle Raheim,
Have A JOOD Birthday!
I Love You,
Destiny

Raheim grinned. "This is really sweet."

"So, how does it feel to officially be in your thirties?"

"Uh . . . I don't know yet."

"Still trying to get a feel for it, huh?"

"Yeah."

"Mmm-hmm. Welcome to the club."

"It . . . it seems like only yesterday I was *twenty*-one. And
now . . . I found my first gray hair the other day."

"You did? Where?"

Raheim leaned forward, pointing to it.

Mitchell laughed. "You call *that* a gray hair? That's not even
a follicle. When you've got it like I do, then we can talk."

"Your hair has grown a lot."

"And *grayed* a lot."

It had. Raheim always wondered if *he* was responsible for
that. "You wear it well."

"The locks or the gray?"

"Both." And he meant it. Not everyone could.

"Thanks."

"Welcome."

Errol appeared. "Hay, Dad."

"Hay, son."

They shook with their fists and hugged.

"Thanks for coming."

"Thanks for askin' me to."

"I see you're finally *red*-y," Mitchell observed. He was wear-

ing the very bright fire-engine-red shirt Mitchell had purchased for his birthday.

Errol laughed. "I am. How do I look?" He double-backed,
posing.

"You look jood."

"Thanks."

"Did you spray your entire body with that cologne?" That
was one of his other presents: a bottle of Bijan.

"No."

"It sure does smell like it."

"All it took was two sprits."

"I *love* that shirt, son," Raheim admired.

"Thanks."

"Maybe you'll let me borrow it."

Errol smiled at Mitchell. "You might not have to."

"What do you mean?" Raheim quizzed.

"Uh, did everyone e-mail you back their RSVP?" Mitchell
interrupted.

"Yup."

"And they know if they don't have the e-vite, they don't
get in?"

"Yup."

"And that they can't bring any tagalongs?"

"Yup."

"And that—"

"—there will be no drugs or alcohol of any kind allowed?
Yes. Dad, will you man the door?"

"Sure."

"Cool. I'll get the list for you." Errol hustled out.

"I have something for you." Mitchell went into the hall
closet. He returned with a rectangular box wrapped in gold paper and tied with white ribbon. "Happy birthday."

Raheim studied it—and not because he was trying to figure
out what it was. It had been five years since he received a birth-

day gift from Mitchell. Mitchell's never forgotten his birthday, though: Raheim's always gotten a card and/or a phone call, and Raheim has saved each one of those Hallmarks and voice-mail messages (little does he know that Mitchell has saved all of *his* birthday acknowledgments, too).

"You *can* open it," Mitchell advised.

He did. It was the same shirt Errol had on. "Wow. Thanks."

It was a look of joy Mitchell never thought he'd see again. It made him beam too. "You're welcome."

"Like father, like son, huh?"

"Indeed."

Errol returned with Monroe and Sidney. He handed his father the list. "Here ya go, Dad."

"Mr. R, if anybody gets outta hand, we can take care of 'em." Monroe winked, elbowing Raheim in the side.

"The only thing you're gonna be takin' care of is your appetite," predicted Sidney.

"That, too." Monroe eyed the food laid out on the island. "Whoa! Turkey meatballs!"

"You won't be eating anything until the party begins," Mitchell informed him.

"Dad, can I get a picture with you?"

"Of course."

Sidney clicked it. They all viewed it on the digital camera's screen.

"Very nice," observed Mitchell.

"Yeah. Y'all could be twins," added Monroe.

Father and son grinned.

The rain didn't stop and it didn't stop the show—the party still got under way at seven sharp. It was reminiscent of so many hip-hop videos: honeyz in various states of hoochie undress (halters, minis, and spaghetti-strapped formfitting dresses) on the left and fellaz thugged up (Timbs, tanks, jeans, jerseys, and sweatsuits) or casual down (button-down shirts, chinos, and cowrie-shell-draped necks) on the right. There were an even number of boyz and girlz (forty guests in all), and they came in every color (and noncolor) of the rainbow (mainly Black and Latino, with others from places as far as Tokyo, Bangladesh, and Saudi Arabia, and the lone "wigga" and "wiggette"—who did not come or leave together). The "10 percent" was also in the house: a female couple (serving butch and femme), and two SGL males, both falling under the "homo-thug" category. Most were Tech students, some were from the neighborhood, and a few ventured from Harlem (such as Precious, D.C.'s daughter, and Anjelica, Angel's daughter, both escorted by Precious's older cousin, Juwan). After playing some "mingling music" (i.e., catchy midtempo tunes by the likes of Jaheim, Tweet, and Whitney Houston that had a few folks on the floor but that most grooved to in place while chatting with others, drinking, and eating) for about an hour, the deejay announced: "A'ight, y'all, it's time to really get this party started right!"

And the room went up as he spun 50 Cent's "In da Club." Everybody chanted "We gonna party like it's your birthday," surrounding Errol as he did just that, rocking the floor. And on every other song, he continued to be THE STAR. The ladies were literally pushing one another out of the way to dance with him. Monroe had to run interference several times, taking one by the hand and usually leaving two to duke it out. There was a little eye-rollin', teeth-suckin', neck-twistin', and hand-wavin,' but no catfights. But some didn't mind sharing—one would work him in the front while the other took the back (and if they were really in a generous mood, switch places during the song).

Max would have none of that. Her full first name was Max-ine. She danced with him the most during the night—five times—and did so solo. She made sure she had him up against a wall so that no one could cut in on her action—and she gave Errol a *lot* of action. She had a lot of breast and a lot of ass to shimmy, shake, and shove in his face and his crotch. And if they were giving out awards for the most scandalous outfit of the night, she would've won by a landslide: her dress (if one could call it that) was really a two-piece leopard-print bikini with a matching skirt wrap that left her entire left thigh exposed, and her stiletto heels were in the same style. Every other unattached straight guy at the party (including the deejay and his two-man crew) wanted to take her for a grind, but she turned them all down.

But Max didn't have a "special dance" with Errol.

"Before we cut the birthday cake," he began, "I want to invite two young ladies to the floor: Precious and Anjelica."

They were surprised and touched by their being selected. After complying with his request, he took the hand of each. "We grew up together. Our fathers were . . . still are the best of friends. So we're like family. I'm so happy they are here tonight—our lives have taken some unexpected turns, but we've always known that no matter how crazy things got, we could depend on each other." He was no doubt referring to Laticia, Precious's mother, who almost died in a car crash three years ago, and Yvonne, Anjelica's maternal grandmother, who turned up missing on 9/11. A token-booth clerk at the World Trade Center train station on the E line, she was found by Raheim and Angel at Bellevue Hospital a month later, burned over 20 percent of her body. Under Raheim's mother's watchful eye, she's made a complete recovery.

"Everybody ought to have angels in their lives—and I'm lucky to have two." Errol kissed both of their hands.

Everyone ooh'ed and aah'ed. Precious was on the verge of tears; Anjelica was already crying.

"So I dedicate this song to them." He nodded toward the deejay. With his arm wrapped around each, he rocked them to TLC's "Turntable." Precious rested her head near his right shoulder blade while Anjelica continued to boo-hoo on his chest. By the end of the song, several others were teary-eyed—including Mitchell and Raheim.

By the time eleven o'clock rolled around, only Sidney, Monroe, Juliette, her best friend Ananda, and Max remained. Sidney took Juliette and Ananda home; Monroe went along for the cab ride so Sidney wouldn't have to ride the A train back by himself (and so he could continue to holla at Ananda). After walking Max to her car and giving her a passionate kiss good night, Errol came down to the basement, where Mitchell was clearing up the cups and plates and Raheim was folding up the chairs.

"So, did you have a jood time?" Mitchell asked.

"I had a *better*-than-jood time. Thanks." He bear-hugged Mitchell from behind.

Mitchell smiled. "You're welcome."

Errol rested his chin on Mitchell's right shoulder. "Any turkey meatballs left?"

"I was able to hide a few from Monroe. They're on the bottom shelf in the fridge."

"Cool. I'm gonna eat before I leave."

"Then you better do it now. Monroe and Sidney will be back soon. You still have to shower and change." Errol and Sidney would be spending the night at Monroe's.

"Okay." Errol walked over to his father. "I'm so glad you came, Dad." He embraced him.

Raheim hadn't heard that sentiment in some time. He squeezed him *tight*. "Me, too."

"You're gonna stick around until Roe and Sid come back," Errol presumed.

"Of course," Raheim assured him.

"Jood," he grinned. He grabbed the trash bag and bounced upstairs.

"That was one *live* party," Raheim observed. "I wish I had a party like that when I was his age. Ha, I'd love to have a party like that at *any* age."

Mitchell didn't respond.

Raheim could tell something was up. "What's wrong?"

"What do you mean?"

"Somethin's botherin' you, Lit—" He caught himself; he looked away, a little embarrassed.

Mitchell wasn't bothered by his slip of the tongue; he smiled to himself. "Well, I would expect most of the guests to be a couple of years older than him, since he's in the eleventh grade. But nineteen?"

"Who was nineteen?"

"Maxine."

"How you know?"

"I asked her."

Raheim laughed to himself. That's just like Mitchell to be overly concerned. It's one of the things he's always loved about him. "There ain't no law that says he can't hang with folks three or four years older than him. Besides, he don't look—or act—fifteen," he argued.

"I suppose. But coming to the party is one thing; giving an inappropriate gift is another."

"Inappropriate?"

"Yes. You think it's appropriate for a nineteen-year-old woman to give a fifteen-year-old boy underwear?"

Errol had opened his gifts while the cake was being served. Raheim thought the boxers were from his mother.

"She ain't a woman," Raheim said.

"Okay. A nineteen-year-old *young lady*."

"She a teenager."

"Maybe in number. In the eyes of the law she's an adult, and he isn't. Don't you think it's odd that of all the things she could buy him—a CD, a book, a shirt, even some socks—she chose *that*? It makes you wonder."

"Wonder what?"

"You know what. If he and Max are having sex. Why else would she buy him that?"

"That don't mean they havin' sex. Now, if she bought him a six-pack of *condoms* . . ." Raheim chuckled.

Mitchell frowned. "Okay, let's say it was your fifteen-year-old *daughter*, and a nineteen-year-old teenage boy gave her some Victoria's Secret lace panties as a present."

"*What?*" Raheim shrieked.

"Now, how did I know that *that* was the reaction I'd receive . . . ?" Mitchell smirked.

"Some grown man buyin'—"

"And *he's* grown, while the female in that same position would be a *teenager*?"

Raheim thought about it. "I see whatcha sayin'."

"It shouldn't and doesn't make a difference what the genders are."

"A'ight. I'll ask him about it."

Raheim knocked on Errol's door.

"Yes?"

"Can I come in?"

"Sure."

He entered. "Hay."

"Hay." Errol was sitting at the foot of his bed, putting on sweatsocks. He had on a pair of boxers Max just gave him (white with red hearts).

Raheim surveyed his room: posters of Aaliyah (who was over his bed), Ashanti, Janet, Halle, J-Lo, The Rock, Alex Rodriguez, Barry Bonds, Kobe Bryant, Tiger Woods, the comic strip *The*

Boondocks and the TV show *Justice League* covered his walls, which were a chocolate brown. A dartboard with a black-and-white snapshot of a smiling George W. Bush (which was full of holes) was tacked to his closet door. A periodic-table-of-elements chart hung above a maple bookcase; encyclopedias occupied its bottom two shelves, and several dozen copies of *American Scientist, Astrology,* and *Macworld* were stacked on top. On his desk was the Power Mac G5 his father purchased for Christmas (images of last month's lunar eclipse and Michael P. Armstrong, who died in the Columbia shuttle crash in February, flashed on the twenty-three-inch display); to its right were the Harry Potter and Lord of the Rings books and their DVD companions, *The Sorcerer's Stone, The Chamber of Secrets,* and *The Fellowship of the Ring,* which were in a case along with *Spider-Man; The Mask of Zorro; The Iron Giant; Chicken Run; The Matrix; The Scorpion King; Crouching Tiger, Hidden Dragon; The Tuskegee Airmen;* and *Soul of the Game* (the last two he received as birthday gifts from his grandfather last weekend). On top of his dresser were photos of him with his mother; his grandfather; Mitchell; Destiny; Monroe and Sidney; and Neil de Grasse Tyson, director of the Hayden Planetarium at the American Museum of Natural History, who had given a lecture at Brooklyn Tech earlier in the week.

Raheim pointed to that last picture. "Did you get to talk to him yesterday?"

"Yeah. He said I could get an internship at the planetarium next spring."

"You must've made an impression. Will it be a paid one?"

"I don't know. I was so excited when he mentioned it, I forgot to ask. But it doesn't matter. Just being there with him would be payment enough." He grabbed a pair of black jeans off the bed and slid into them.

Raheim made out the drawing over his bed: it was a piece he'd done on a night they were celebrating their birthdays. He got closer to it. *Li'l Brotha Man—1994*. He smiled. "I wondered what happened to that."

"I found it in a box, with a lot of your other work. Grandma framed it."

Raheim looked over at his nightstand; there was the framed *Your World* cover with Errol sitting on his daddy's lap as he blew out his candles at age five (Raheim was surprised to still see this displayed on the mantel over the fireplace in the great room, along with one of Raheim holding Destiny a few hours after she was born), and a photo of them that was taken when Raheim received his GED last year. As he glanced back at Errol, he caught the glint of color on his very flat, ripped abs.

Errol noticed him squinting. "Oh, I got the tattoos."

"Ah. Did your mom see them?"

"Just one of them."

As Raheim made out the one on his left side, he was shocked to see "Dad" also spelled out in a heart with an arrow through it. "Wow. Nice."

"Thanks."

Caught off guard by this tribute, Raheim stumbled over his thoughts. "Uh, you've got a jood-lookin' setup."

"Thanks."

"Uh, can we talk?"

"Sure."

Raheim plopped down in his desk chair.

Errol sat back on the bed. He put on a red St. John's University T-shirt. "It's about Max, right?" he guessed.

"Yeah. Where did y'all meet?"

"At a college fair in April. She'll be a sophomore at NYU this fall."

"Ah. And . . . how does she know what size you wear?"

"She asked me."

"Well, exactly what . . . how . . ."

"Yeah, she wants me."

"And you?"

"The feeling is mutual. I mean, come on, Dad: Look at her. She's what B2K and Diddy are singin' about in 'Bump Bump Bump.' "

"So, you two haven't . . ."

"No."

"Do y'all plan to?"

"I have no plans to, unless she ends up being my wife. I'm saving myself."

"For what?"

"For when I get married."

Raheim's eyes widened. "Really?"

"Yup."

"So, you a virgin?"

"Yup."

"You've never had sex?"

"Nope."

"*Never?*"

"Yup, never."

He was . . . well, *shocked.* "*Really?*"

Errol chuckled. "Yeah, *really.*"

"Uh . . . when did you decide you would do this?"

"On my birthday."

"And how. . . . what brought you to . . . make this kind of choice?"

"I want my first time to be with the woman I love, not just some female I like or lust."

"You're not gonna be intimate with any woman until your wedding night?"

"We can be intimate—kiss and stuff."

"And stuff?"

"Yeah. I can be with her without *being* with her. We can hold and caress each other. Smooch."

"Have you done those things with any young ladies?"

"With a few."

"How many is a few?"

"Like three or four."

Raheim replayed Errol's dance sessions at the party with Max. "Don'tcha think doin' those things—especially if it's with a young lady that looks like Max—could be dangerous?"

"What do you mean?"

"It could put your plan in jeopardy. You start holdin' and caressin' and then smoochin' and kissin' and then feelin' and rubbin,' and the next thing you know, y'all are bumpin' and grindin',"

"I know when to put on the brakes."

"Are you datin' Max?"

"No."

"Are you datin' anybody right now?" Raheim knew Errol had been on a few study dates to the library and caught a movie and grabbed some pizza with several young ladies, but up until now hadn't had a steady girlfriend.

"No. There are a few girls tryin' to holla, but I got too much on my plate to get caught up or tied down. It takes a lot of energy to deal with females."

Raheim laughed to himself. *It takes a lot of energy to deal with the men, too.* "And . . . you plan on bein' a *total* virgin until you get married?"

He chuckled. "Yeah, Dad. Unlike some of my peers, I do know that oral sex *is* sex."

He read my mind . . .

Now, how do I ask him about this? "You haven't had sex, but have you . . . do you . . ."

Errol's eyebrows rose. "Whack my wood?"

They laughed. Raheim noticed how similar in volume and texture their laughs were.

"I have and I do," Errol admitted. "Just because I'm a virgin doesn't mean I can't have sex with myself."

"You want your wife to be a virgin, too?"

"That'd be a plus. But if I fall in love with a woman who isn't, I wouldn't hold that against her. So long as she doesn't hold my being a virgin against me."

"Do your boyz know you a virgin?"

"Yeah. They're cool about it. Sid is like a born-again virgin."

"A born-again virgin?"

"Yeah. He's had sex a few times, but now he plans to wait until he marries Juliette. And Roe is glad one of us is a virgin 'cause there can only be one Mack in the crew, and *he's* it."

"Ha, from what I could see, you was the Mack tonite. Those young ladies were all over you."

"You get perks when it's your birthday." He grinned.

"Does Max know?"

"Nope. If she did, she'd be trying to change *that* situation!" They laughed again. *There goes that echo...*

"There's gonna be a lot of Maxes out there. Sure you gonna be able to hold out?"

"Yeah. It's about being true to myself."

"And there's gonna be fellas who won't be as understandin' as Roe and Sid. They're gonna rib you. I remember when I was your age." And *Raheim* was the fella who did much of the ribbin', since he started sexin' at thirteen. Raheim was so sure Errol would also begin dippin' at an early age that he gave Errol "the birds and the bees" talk just before he entered high school, at twelve—at the end of which Raheim demonstrated, with a banana, how to place on a condom.

"I'm not concerned with what people think. All that matters is that I'm comfortable with it."

If only I'd been as confident and self-assured when I was fifteen.

"And what if you're my age or older and you still haven't found that *one*? It might be harder as the years go by to keep that promise to yourself."

Errol shrugged. "It can be done. A. C. Green did it. Besides, sex is so overrated. I'm interested in making love. And if I get that frustrated, I can always wave my magic wand."

Raheim shook his head in admiration. "Wow, son. I'm proud of you. There aren't many young bruthas like you out here takin' a vow like that."

"Thanks. But I think there are. It's just that the ones having sex get all the press. I know bruthas at Tech who are virgins— and some of them try to convince everybody they do it all the time."

"How can you tell they're lyin'?"

"Not only are there not enough hours in a day for them to do it as much as they say they do, they haven't been alive long enough to have experienced all they say they have. But enough about *my* sex life: let's talk about *yours*."

Raheim did a double take. "Pardon me?"

"Come on, Dad. I know you and what's-his-name broke up."

What's-his-name. Errol had never called Simon that to his face, but whenever he talked to Raheim about him, it was always . . . "How is *what's-his-name*?" "You out with *what's-his-name*?" "Is *what's-his-name* there?" "Grandma said you and *what's-his-name* came by the restaurant the other day." Raheim always figured that he refused to speak Simon's name because he'd have to accept Raheim's not being with Mitchell anymore.

"How did you find out?" *Like I don't know . . .*

"Grandpa."

Of course. "I guess jood news travels fast."

"*Is* it jood news?"

"It probably is for you."

"Why would it be jood news for me?"

"I thought you never liked Simon."

"That's not true."

"It's not?"

"It's not that I didn't like *him*. I didn't like him for *you*."

Of course. "Well, we were ... we couldn't ... I ... he ..."

"You don't have to explain what happened. How have you been handling it?"

"It's been ... kinda rough. I ... still care for him. Hmmph, this is kinda weird."

"What is?"

"Talkin' to my son about breakin' up with my ... friend." Raheim still hadn't come up with the right word to describe the men in his life.

"Ha, you were much more than *friends*!" Errol corrected him.

They laughed again. It was like music.

"Are you *still* friends?"

"Just bein' friends right now ... that would be difficult."

Errol contemplated his next question; it was as if he was afraid what the answer would be. "Are you dating?"

"No."

Errol wasn't doing it on the outside, but Raheim knew he was smiling on the inside.

"Uh, thanks for askin', son. I appreciate that."

Errol nodded. "You're welcome."

"Well, I'll let you finish gettin' ready." Raheim rose to leave.

"Oh, don't forget these." Errol went over to his desk and took something off the printer. He handed them to his father. They were copies of the pictures Sidney snapped: Errol and his father before the party began and Raheim with Mitchell as things were winding down.

Raheim grinned. "Wow. These are beautiful." He recalled Max's reaction, learning he was Errol's father. "We *could* be brothers."

"Yeah." Errol play punched him in the right arm. "But *you* would be the *older* one."

They laughed again. This time it was lighter but just as lovely.

Raheim trudged into the kitchen, where Mitchell was wrapping up leftovers.

"So?" Mitchell queried.

Raheim filled him in.

"*Well*..." Mitchell mused. "Your son never ceases to impress me."

"Listenin' to him, it's hard to believe he *is* my son."

"What do you mean?"

"It's like I'm lookin' in a mirror, sixteen years ago. But he's doing everything I didn't do. Graduatin' from high school. Goin' to college. *Stayin'* a virgin. I guess he's really learned from my mistakes."

"*Your* mistakes? You think he's pursuing his own life according to how you haven't lived yours? He's doing everything you would want him to do. Besides, if *you* had stayed a virgin, *he* wouldn't be here."

Raheim sighed. "Yeah."

Mitchell noticed the printouts in his hand; he reached for them. "You two *could* be twins"—he looked up at him—"if it weren't for that single gray hair."

They laughed.

When Sidney and Monroe returned around midnight, Raheim offered to drive them to Monroe's house—which was only three blocks away. They accepted—Errol, so he could spend a little more time with his dad; Sidney, to continue their discussion about Raheim's being on one of his favorite shows, *Forensic Files;* and Monroe, so he could finally say he rode in a Benz (a 1991 model, it's the only piece of property Raheim owns; the fact that he got the car at a police auction last year for $6,300 when his own car was repossessed was not lost on him). Raheim unlocked the doors as they were all walking out of the gate.

"Raheim?" Mitchell called.

Raheim turned. "Yeah?"

Mitchell stepped out of the doorway. "Uh . . . my mother and Anderson will be coming over for dinner tomorrow. They'll be bringing Destiny home. I . . . I know Destiny would love to see you."

Raheim didn't think about it for a second. "What time?"

"Say, four o'clock?"

"Should I bring somethin'?"

"No."

"A'ight. I'll see you tomorrow."

"Jood. Have a jood night."

"You, too."

sunday,
june 8, 2003

H ello?"

"Mornin', Mitch."

" 'Chelle?" It was Michelle Snipes, Mitchell's former coworker at *Your World* magazine. Mitchell looked at the clock above the top oven: 11:05 A.M. "What are you doin' up this early on a Sunday?"

"I know, right? Chile, I'd usually be rollin' over about now. The only thing that could get me out of bed this early is a patient. I had an emergency root canal." She had realized her dream of becoming a dentist in 2000 and has had her own practice in Los Angeles the past two years.

"He or she must've been in a lot of pain if they couldn't wait until Monday morning."

"Uh-huh, and their pain was my pleasure."

"But of course. Who was it?"

"Now, you know I can't reveal that information . . ." She's managed to rope a few celebrity clients, but won't disclose their names. She will, however, give him clues, like . . . "They were in *Ocean's 11*," "They just won a Daytime Emmy," "They were recently arrested for drunk driving," or "They just got out of rehab" (given where she was, the latter two could be almost anybody).

Today's hint: "They were on *Three's Company*."

"Well, it can't be Suzanne Somers—her teeth are as straight and blond as her hair," Mitchell argued. "Are you still in the office?"

"Yeah. I'm 'bout to leave, get myself some breakfast. I'm sure you must be about done eating yours. I hear Mrs. Karen Clark-Sheard in the background."

"I haven't even started it and probably won't. I've been so busy with Sunday dinner."

"Oh? What's on the menu?"

"A turkey with stuffing, a ham, greens, peas and rice, baked macaroni and cheese, candied yams, corn bread, and chocolate cake for dessert."

"*Damn*. What are you *not* cookin'? Isn't smothered chicken your usual second Sunday—*uh-huh*."

"What?"

"You *finally* invited him to dinner."

He inhaled. "Yes."

"*Hallelujah!*" she shouted. "There could only be one reason why you'd be slavin' in that Emeril kitchen. I take it things went very *jood* last night?"

"Yeah. The party went off without a hitch."

"I wasn't talkin' about the party. Is he still asleep, or standing just a few feet away?"

"He's not here. He didn't spend the night."

"Ah. How long you been up cookin'?"

"Since five."

"Oooh," she purred. "He musta put some spell on you for you to prepare a Thanksgiving feast for two."

As it turns out, Raheim *did* put a spell on him. It wasn't seeing him for the first time in almost six months (Raheim attended Destiny's birthday party last December), but Raheim's aroma that worked some magic. It's a natural scent Raheim exudes that is . . . *hypnotic*. It actually turned Mitchell off during the years they became estranged, and he never noticed it after their breakup. He also didn't remember smelling it last year. But last *night*? It was so intoxicating that Mitchell made up that excuse about Destiny so he could invite Raheim back and *breathe* him in some more.

Mitchell didn't admit this to Michelle, though; he was embarrassed (yet tickled) by his reaction. "No, my mother, stepfather, and Destiny will be here. And Errol, depending on what time he comes back."

"So you're gonna let your mom and Destiny do the interrogation. *Jood* plan. And since you brought up my future husband: Did E. enjoy himself?"

"He had a ball. Those girls just couldn't get enough of him."

"I can understand why."

"But one young lady had his attention for most of the evening. She goes to NYU."

"Ah, my alma mater. And how old is she?"

"Nineteen."

"See: he *does* have a thing for older women."

"Yes, older women, not *old* women." He snickered.

"Don't get it twisted, okay? Three more years and he is *mine*. We can have a double wedding; I'll be marrying the son and you, the father."

"Maybe you should set your sights on the *grand*father."

"Ain't he like fifty years old? I don't want a man who carries a senior citizens' discount card. You gotta get 'em *before* they get set in their ways. I'd be spending half the time frustrated over stuff he couldn't change if he wanted to, and the other half fighting with him over things he can but won't."

"Don't you know you're supposed to accept folks just the way they are?"

"Where you hear that, in a song? I got another one for ya: Like Anita, I don't believe in fairy tales. Forget the shining armor; just give me the knight!"

They laughed.

"And what time are you expecting *your* knight?"

"Four o'clock."

"Well, have a jood time. And have an even *jooder* time after the kids are put to bed."

"He can't spend the night."

"Why not?"

"Because it's way too early to be even thinking about something like that."

"My dear, you two have a very long history of *doing* something like that."

"Yes, we do, but it's a history. Besides, I've never had a man spend the night with the kids in the house."

"There's a first time for everything. Besides, he ain't a stranger."

"Still . . . I don't know if Destiny is old enough to shoulder something like this."

"Ha, now you sound like one of those Concerned Caucasian Women for America. *Puh-leeze*. You don't think Destiny knows her father is in love with her uncle Raheim? It's written all over your face whenever you talk about him. And Raheim the Third ain't gonna be bothered. You think it's a coincidence that he decided to have his *first* birthday party in five years at his godfather's house and asked his father—*not* his mother, *not* his stepfather, *not* his grandfather—to help chaperon? They'd be surprised if he *didn't* spend the night."

"Before we even think of going there . . . a lot has to be said. And a lot has to happen."

"Well, you can play it safe; just know you don't have to. You two were meant to be—and will be again. Even Miss Cleo could predict that!"

O kay. What about this?"

It was two o'clock and Raheim was *still* trying on outfits. Unsatisfied with anything in his own closet, he was now going through his father's.

And, as he had done in his son's room, the elder Rivers stood back, amused by the whole spectacle. "It looks jood," he said for the tenth time.

"Just jood?"

"*Just* jood?"

"Yeah. Just jood ain't jood enough, Pop."

"It ain't?"

"Nah. I wanna look better than jood."

He chuckled. "Son, everything you tried on in the past hour has been better-than-jood."

"You just sayin' that."

"No, I'm not. You think I'd let you walk out of this house lookin' wrecked?"

Raheim eyed something in his father's closet. He pulled it out. He held it up. "What about this?"

"My blue suit? Don't you think that'll be a little too dressy? You're not meeting with the president of Paramount Pictures. It's just dinner."

"It ain't just dinner, Pop."

"It ain't?"

"Nah. This is . . . it's different."

"How?"

"It . . . it just is. The way he asked me. The look in his eyes."
*And the way he used Destiny as a security blanket, the way I used
to with Li'l Brotha Man....*

His father shrugged. "Okay."

"You don't believe me?"

"I *do* believe you. I can tell by the look in *your* eyes that you
heard what you heard and saw what you saw. And I know you're
excited—you woke me up early this mornin' singin' that song,
over and over and *over* again. You ain't Gladys *or* a Pip."

"Sorry," Raheim said, a little embarrassed.

"You don't have to be sorry; just be careful. I know you an-
ticipate this leadin' to somethin', but . . . just slow your roll."

Raheim was shocked he even knew that phrase.

And the elder Rivers could tell. "Your father may be older
but he ain't *ancient*."

They smiled.

"You've been through a lot. And you just got out of a relationship."

"You're the one who said I need to date more," Raheim reminded him.

"Yes, date, not *mate*. You're already lookin' forward to a rec-
onciliation. But that kind of reunion ain't gonna happen just
like that."

"I know it ain't gonna happen just like that."

"And the reality is . . . it might not happen."

"It's gonna happen." Raheim pouted, hanging the suit
back up.

His father approached him, putting his left hand on Raheim's right shoulder. "Son, if you get your hopes up and it

doesn't come off, you'll be crushed. I don't wanna see you get
hurt. Besides, *I* want it to happen, too. That'll mean you'll finally be moving out of here."

"You tryin' to get rid of me?"

"Tryin'? I thought I was succeedin'." He winked.

Their doorbell rang.

He playfully pushed Raheim out the room. "*You* get that.
This way I know you're not trying on something else."

Raheim trudged up the hall. He looked through the peep-
hole. He opened the door.

"Hay, Amelia."

"Hey, Junior."

They hugged and kissed.

"How are you?" she asked.

"I'm jood. You?"

"I'm jood, too. Ooh, I *love* that shirt."

"You should. You bought it for Pop."

"Oh. You look even jooder in it. And I'm sure Mitchell will
love *you* in it."

"You think so?"

"Definitely. Are you nervous?"

"A little."

"Well, you should be. But that's a jood thing. It'll keep you
focused and on your toes. Just don't start trippin' over your feet
and knockin' shit over. That will not make a jood impression."

"Ha, I won't."

"Is your father ready?"

The elder Rivers appeared with his bowling bag. "I am.
Hey, baby."

"Hey, TB." She calls him TB, short for Teddy Bear, since he's
six inches taller and almost a hundred pounds heavier. They
kissed.

"Have a jood time, son."

"I will."

"And, please, don't spend another hour goin' through our closets."

"I won't. Jood luck today."

"Thanks. But we know luck ain't got nothin' to do with it." He trumped up his chest.

"That's why I love this man—he's so humble." Amelia turned to her man. "Uh, aren't you going to wear a jacket?"

Pop Rivers frowned. "What for?"

"It's raining," Amelia matter-of-factly stated.

He shrugged. "I've had worse things fall on me." He opened the door.

"And when you catch the flu and have to miss the championships . . . ?"

He stopped. He turned. "I'll get a jacket." He made his way up the hall.

She looked at Raheim. "Right."

"Son, I'm gonna borrow your light blue breaker."

"A'ight."

"What would that man do without me?" she boasted.

Raheim chuckled. "You two act like husband and wife."

"And that's how it's gonna stay. Girlfriend is *not* messin' up a jood thing by gettin' married again." She's been divorced—twice. "Did you pack a toothbrush?"

"Huh?"

She put her left hand on her hip. "I'm sure I don't have to explain that."

She didn't; he got it. "He only asked me over for *dinner*."

"Uh-huh—and *you'll* be the dessert."

aheim rang the downstairs bell at 3:59 P.M. Mitchell opened the door. "Hi."

"Hay. These are for you." He presented him with a dozen roses—four white, four yellow, four red.

It had been years since a man had given Mitchell flowers (and, yeah, that man had been Raheim). "You didn't have to do that. Thank you." He beamed.

The look on his face was something Raheim hadn't seen in a long time—and one he never thought he'd see again. He beamed, too. "You're welcome."

"Come on in."

As soon as he stepped into the house, Raheim caught a whiff of the food; it was heaven. "Somethin' smells *real* jood."

I could say the same thing about you... "I hope it'll taste jood."

He followed Mitchell into the kitchen. "I'm sure it will."

Mitchell filled the aqua-blue vase on the island with water. "I *love* that shirt."

It was canary yellow; Raheim's ensemble also included black slacks and shoes. He'd known Mitchell would love it. "Thanks."

"I'm sure your son will want to borrow it."

"He'll have to ask his grandfather."

"Mmm . . . loving bright-colored clothes must be genetic."

"Uh, yeah."

Mitchell arranged the flowers, admiring them, while Raheim admired him.

"Would you like another cranberry-apple mix?"

"That'd be cool."

As he made his drink, Mitchell eyed the black leather clutch under Raheim's arm. "That's a handsome case."

Raheim had forgotten all about it. "Oh, thanks. I've got a script in here. It's the lead in a movie."

"Really?"

"Yeah. I was hopin' you'd read it. Tell me what you think."

It had been a *loooong* time since he asked Mitchell for guidance in his career, for his opinion on any decisions he planned to make—and it felt *jood* to be asked. "I'd love to." He handed Raheim his juice.

"Thanks." Raheim handed him the case.

They stood in stone-smiling-silence for several seconds. The bell rang.

"Excuse me." Mitchell placed the case on the hall vanity as he made his way to the door. Raheim guzzled down his juice.

"Hi, Daddy!" Destiny had her arms up to hug him.

Mitchell knelt to receive it. "Hi, Sugar Plum. Oh, I missed you . . ."

"I missed you, too, times two!"

"How was your weekend?"

"It was . . ." Destiny caught a glimpse of the figure standing in the hall. Her entire face glowed; her mouth opened and she breathed in a sigh of joy. *"Uncle Raheim!"* Her arms stretched wide, she zoomed into his arms.

He scooped her up. "Hay, Baby Doll. How you been?"

She lovingly clutched him by the neck. "I been jood. How *you* been?"

He chuckled. "I been jood. Thank you for my card."

"You're welcome. You liked it?"

"I *loved* it."

"Jood. I'm glad. Ooh, I saw you on TV yesterday."

"You did?"

"Uh-huh. With Janet Jackson. In a video. Gran'ma said you was in Africa."

"Yeah, I was."

"It looks so pretty. Was that a *real* elephant?"

"Sure was."

"Wow. It looks so big. Did you get to touch it?"

"No."

"Oh."

"You like elephants?"

"Uh-huh."

"Well, maybe one day we can go to the zoo to see some."

"Okay. I would like that."

"Well." It was Mitchell's aunt Ruth. "I decide to surprise my nephew and *I* get a surprise. How are you, darling?"

Raheim put Destiny down to give Ruth a hug. "I'm jood. And you?"

"Honey, I can't complain. No, scratch that: I *could* complain, but what's the use? It ain't gonna change a thing." She took him in, head to toe and back again. "You are *still* the cutest chocolate thang I've *ever* seen."

Raheim blushed.

Mitchell's mother kissed Raheim on the cheek as they hugged. "Mitchell didn't tell me you'd be here. It's so good to see you."

Destiny took Raheim's left hand. "You mean jood, Gran'ma." She nodded. "Oh, yes. Jood."

Ruth inhaled the aroma. "That food *smells* jood. Is it ready, Honeysuckle?"

"In about fifteen minutes."

"That'll give me just enough time to have an appetizer." She took a pack of Virginia Slims out of her pocket. She looped her arm through Raheim's. "While you and Ann get things ready, Raheim and I can catch up."

"Can I come?" asked Destiny, still holding on to Raheim's left hand.

"No, Sugar Dumplin'," Ruth replied. "This is grown-up talk."

"Oh," she sighed, disappointed.

"You need to get that voice ready. I still wanna hear that song."

"Okay. Uncle Raheim, you have to stay after dinner and hear me sing, too."

"Of course. You know I wouldn't miss that." He pinched her right cheek. She giggled.

"You don't mind if I borrow him for a moment, do you?" Ruth directed toward Mitchell.

"No."

"Where we goin'?" Raheim inquired.

She swiped an ashtray off the hall stand. "The smoking section."

They sat opposite each other on the stoop's top railing.

After some small talk and a picture show of her five-year-old identical-twin grandsons, Ruth cut to the chase. "So . . . how long you been single?"

"What makes you think I'm single?"

"Why else would you be dressed so sharp, havin' dinner with your ex?"

"I could be dressed sharp for Destiny," Raheim argued, unconvincingly.

"Uh-huh. Like, *Destiny* loves the way you look in bright-colored clothes . . . ? How long . . . ?"

"Six months."

"What took you so long?"

"Uh . . . I . . . he . . ."

"Let me guess: You didn't want it to seem like you were on the rebound; you didn't know if he was involved with anyone; and you weren't sure, even if he *wasn't*, he'd be interested."

He looked at her in amazement.

"Honey, I ain't get this age bein' stupid. I had a *feelin'*. I never woulda guessed it would be about you."

"Whatcha mean?"

"It's rare that I am at my sister's on a Sunday—or leave the state of New Jersey. So, when she called to see if I'd take the trip to bring Destiny home, I knew there was a reason why I was supposed to visit. I've been watchin' you."

"Have you?"

"Mmm-hmm. As Billie once crooned, you've changed. I know it's not just an act I've seen on TV. And I'm sure he can see it, too."

I hope she's right . . .

"Goin' through what you went through . . . it must have been hard, without him."

"Yeah."

"I know how tough it can be." She jiggled her cigarette. "I've gone from a pack a day, to one a day, to one a *week*."

"Wow. Congrats."

"Thanks. And I joined the ranks of the divorced four years ago, too."

"Oh. I'm sorry."

"Ain't no need to be sorry about it. I'm not."

"Did you want to get divorced?"

"No."

"Then he wanted to . . . ?"

"No."

"Then why did you?"

"We had to. Sometimes two people may love each other, may

still be *in* love with each other, but love ain't enough to keep them together. You know what I mean?"

I sure do...

"Tweed and I became different people with different journeys to take. And we had to accept that we'd have to take those journeys without each other as husband and wife." She sighed.

"You sound sad about it."

"We were married for thirty-seven years. I was sad to see it end; I still am. But in order for us to be happier, it had to."

"Happier?"

"Yeah. It wasn't that we didn't make each other happy; it was that we both knew we would be happier if we weren't together. And we are. In fact, he's gone on to find happier times: last June, he remarried. And that makes *me* even happier."

"It does?"

"Of course. Just because he's no longer with me doesn't mean he should be *un*happy. Love means you wish that person well no matter what. Just because the union died doesn't mean the love you have for them does."

Amen to that, too...

"Besides, he ain't the only one with somebody new. *I'm* currently seeing a man." She grinned. "A *younger* man."

"Really? How much younger?"

"Try fifteen years."

"Damn. You got your sister beat."

"And after teasin' her so much about Anderson, you know she never lets me forget it."

"What's his name?"

"Freedom. Free for short."

"And I bet he sets you *free*," Raheim joked.

She slapped him on the hand. "Hush yo' mouth, chile. You ain't old enough to have that kind of conversation with me— are you?"

They laughed.

"Let's just say that his mama must've known the power he would unleash, for she gave him the right name. If Tweed could put it down *half* as jood as Free, we might still be married."

"How long y'all been seein' each other?"

"Like two years. I never thought I'd be dating at my age. A *grand*mother." She puffed. "But Free has shown me that, you can think your life—or a part of it—is over, but it ain't over till it's over. Another chapter can start with someone new." She leaned in. "And, sometimes, with someone old."

Destiny tapped on the second-floor door. Ruth opened it. "Yes, Sugar Dumplin'?"

"Daddy says it's time to eat."

"We'll be right in."

"Okay." She went back inside.

Ruth took the last drag on her cigarette. "You two have a lot to work through, a lot to work on. It ain't gonna be easy. And it's gonna get frustratin' and sometimes you're gonna wonder whether it's all worth it. But it is. Love is always worth it."

"I appreciate this. Thanks, Miss Ruth."

"Honey, please, call me *Aunt* Ruth. Your son is practically my great-stepnephew—if there is such a thing." She stood up. "So, are you ready for the third degree from your ex-but-soon-to-be-once-again mother-in-law?"

"I suppose."

"She's gonna have a lot of questions for you. She'll be trusting you with her son *and* her daughter this time. And that's why I wanted us to have this chance to talk. I won't be able to get a word in once she starts." She stood up. "But don't you worry: I got your back."

After washing up, Ruth and Raheim came into the dining area. She gawked at the spread. "Am I dressed for this?"

Mitchell placed a platter of ham on the table. "What do you mean?"

"I have on an old housedress. I didn't know I was comin' to Thanksgiving dinner. The only things missin' are the cranberry sauce and the pumpkin pie."

"Oh, Ruth," Ann said, filling their glasses with iced tea. "We do have a lot to be thankful for." Ann glanced at Destiny. "Don't we, Sweetie Pie?"

"Uh-huh," Destiny agreed.

"And what is a woman with hypertension supposed to eat?" Ruth asked.

"Mmm . . ." Mitchell pondered. "Well, the greens were made with turkey. The stuffing is made with whole-wheat bread. And I used vegetable oil for the peas and rice."

"And you can eat the yams. They have raisins in them," added Destiny.

"I'm sorry, Aunt Ruth. If I had known you were coming, I would've made a garden salad, too."

"It's all right, Honeysuckle. I'll just have small portions."

As Raheim pulled out the chair next to Ruth, Destiny grabbed his right wrist. "No, Uncle Raheim. You sit over here, next to me." She pulled him to the other side of the table.

Mitchell sat at the head, turning to Destiny. "Would you like to say grace?"

"Okay." She took her father's right hand and Raheim's left. Her grandmother took her father's left and Ruth's right. Raheim and Ruth completed the circle. They all bowed their heads.

"God is great, God is *jood*"—she squeezed Raheim's hand on the emphasis—"thank You for our food, a-men."

"Amen," everyone repeated.

"Raheim, would you carve the turkey?" Mitchell requested.

"Sure." Raheim stood, picked up the utensils, and went to carving. "What part do you want, Destiny?"

"A wing, please." He placed it on her plate. "Thank you."

"You're welcome."

"You can give me a leg, honey," Ruth informed him.

Ann surveyed Ruth's plate as she passed it to Raheim. "I thought you said you were going to have small portions?"

"Those *are* small portions."

"Heaping tablespoons are not small portions."

"They were hardly heaping."

Ann motioned toward Destiny's plate, which Mitchell was fixing. "A couple of teaspoons of each would've been more appropriate, Ruth."

"I'd like to *see* the food I'm eating without a magnifying glass." Ruth noticed Mitchell, Raheim, and Destiny staring. "What y'all lookin' at? Haven't you ever seen two sisters argue before?"

Mitchell gave her back her plate. "Yeah, but not you two."

"Oh, please. We've argued more times than I can count."

"We haven't argued that much," Ann protested.

"No? Are you sure *I'm* the older one? I remember things quite differently."

"We've had our disagreements, but you make it sound like we argue all the time."

"I guess that depends on what you mean by *argue*." Ruth winked at Raheim; he picked up that this was her way of keeping the focus off of him.

After "arguing" with her sister for another ten minutes about how much they hadn't argued, Ann zeroed in on her former son-in-law. "If I remember correctly, Raheim, you don't have a sister or brother, do you?"

"That's right."

"I have a brother," Destiny offered, feeling left out.

Everyone stopped chewing.

"You do?" her grandmother asked as Mitchell lowered his head, afraid of what her answer would be.

"Uh-huh. Errol."

They were all embarrassed; what else *would* she say?

Her grandmother nodded. "Why, yes. I forgot. He is."

With that type of familial connection being made by her own granddaughter, Ann couldn't put Raheim through the ringer—not just yet. So the rest of their dinner conversation revolved around Destiny and what she had done with her grandparents over the weekend.

Ann rose with her plate. "Son, that was one terrific meal."

"Thanks, Mom."

"That wasn't a meal, it was a Last Supper," Ruth exclaimed, following her.

Mitchell smiled at Raheim as he finished off his third plate of food. "Would you like some more?"

Raheim placed his fork on the very clean dish in front of him. "No thanks. Everything was *better*-than-jood."

"Thanks. I'm glad you enjoyed it."

"Daddy, may I have my cake now?"

"Yes, you may. Raheim, would you like dessert? Or, should I ask, do you have room for it?"

Raheim rubbed his belly. "I think I got a little room left. Do you have any more of that birthday cake?"

"No, just Destiny's piece. But there's cherry pie. And I made a chocolate cake today."

"That chocolate cake sounds even jooder. I'll have some of that."

"Okay." Mitchell took away Raheim and Destiny's plates.

"Thank you," Raheim and Destiny sang.

"You're both welcome."

"I can share my cake with you, Uncle Raheim."

"That's okay, Baby Doll."

"You sure? I don't mind."

"Well, maybe I'll just have a little taste."

Mitchell was loading some of the dishes Ruth had wiped off

into the dishwasher when his mother stopped him. "We got this."

"You two don't have to—"

"Yes, we do," Ann insisted. "You have company to tend to."

"Thanks. Would either of you like some pie or cake?"

"No, we don't," Ann answered quickly.

Ruth frowned. "See, this is what you have to look forward to: your younger sibling gets to be middle-aged and thinks she can tell *you* what to do."

After gobbling down their dessert, Raheim and Destiny went upstairs to get her karaoke machine (a Christmas gift from her grandparents). It was in her bedroom, which is a little girl's paradise. The wallpaper was powder blue with yellow elephants, and was adorned with posters of Raven-Symone, Little Bill, Blue of Blue's Clues, Dora the Explorer, Bob the Builder, and Clifford the Big Red Dog. A pink doll town house and a giant turquoise elephant were on the right side of her closet door; a five-day clothes-organizer tree was on the left. Her blue personalized items—a rosebud trunk, rocker, and floor pillow—were under her windows. Her small bed, which had drawers around its base, was wrapped in a sky-blue comforter with elephants. There were photos of her with adults on one nightstand (her daddy; her grandparents; her uncles Gene, Babyface, and B.D.; and Raheim) and little people on the other (her "cousins," Elijah and Elliott; her "nephew" and "niece," Gabriel and Garcelle; Korey; Errol, holding her as a baby when he was nine; and a redheaded, freckle-faced white girl). Near the door was a small oak bookcase, with a collection of Blues Clues/Little Bill books and videos on the top shelf and the movies *The Wiz, Cinderella* (Whitney's version), *The Lion King, Dumbo, Babe,* and *Willy Wonka and the Chocolate Factory* on the bottom; and her desk, which had an iMac and an

Oscar the Grouch bank (both passed down to her by Errol; the latter was a birthday present from his uncle D.C. in 1993), as well as a mini-globe and a clear bowl with a single goldfish.

She palmed the bowl, placing her face close. "Hi, Goldie."

Raheim hunched down. "She's pretty."

"Goldie's a *he*, Uncle Raheim, not a *she*."

"Oh. Sorry."

"That's okay. Most people think he is a girl."

"When did you get him?"

"For my birthday. Uncle Gene gave him to me. Daddy says if I take jood care of him, he's gonna get me a clownfish, like the one in *Finding Nemo*."

"Ah. Did you see *Finding Nemo*?"

"Uh-huh."

"Did you like it?"

"Oh, I *loved* it. Did you see it?"

"No."

"Oh. Daddy didn't see it, either. We all can go see it together."

"We?"

"Uh-huh. You, me, and Daddy."

"But you already saw it."

"I wanna see it again."

"You *really* loved it, huh?"

"Uh-huh. It made me cry."

"If it made you sad how can you love it so much?"

"I didn't cry because I was sad; I cried because I was happy."

"Happy about what?"

"That Nemo's daddy found him. Sometimes happy things can make you cry."

"Yeah, they can. Who did you see the movie with?"

"With Errol and Tammy."

"Who's Tammy?"

"She's my best friend."

"Is she the girl in the picture?"

"Uh-huh. She's in kindergarten with me. She cried when Nemo's daddy found him, too."

"Mmm. I guess the movie makes everybody cry."

"Not everybody. Errol didn't cry."

"Ah. I remember when Errol was your age and we went to see *The Lion King*. He cried when Simba's father died."

"Oh. That made me cry, too. Did you cry?"

"No. But it did make me feel sad."

"Well, if you feel sad when we see *Finding Nemo* with Daddy, I can hold your hand." She grabbed it, giving him a preview.

Raheim smiled; she intended to make that movie date with her father happen.

Destiny performed Stacy Lattisaw's "Don't Throw It All Away" in the great room (recently she's tackled another Stacy remake, "Love on a Two-Way Street," and Taral Hicks's version of "Silly"; her signature tunes are Alicia Keys's "Fallin'" and Whitney's "Greatest Love of All," which she'll be performing at her kindergarten graduation in two weeks.) Her father silently reminded her to breathe and provided a little background vocal support. When she hit high notes she stood on her tippy toes, and she had watched enough music videos to know when to sway her body, cock her head, and flail her arms. She had been practicing the song for a month, and while she sounded like Stacy, you could detect her own vocalese.

After she finished, she clutched the mike with both hands against her chest and bowed her head for each audience member—and each one clapped, cheered, and screamed louder than the one before.

Her daddy, though, was too busy bawling like a baby to scream (he did clap). They hugged. She wiped his tears.

"See, Uncle Raheim. I told you you don't have to be sad to cry."

"Yeah. I see."

"Well, I think this is cause for a celebration," announced Ruth. "How about an ice-cream toast?"

"A ice-cream toast?" Destiny queried.

"Yes. We'll all get a spoonful of ice cream and toast you."

"Ooh, I want chocolate and strawberry on my spoon!"

Ruth took her hand. "Me, too."

"Ha, me three," Mitchell concurred, following them into the kitchen.

Ann took Raheim's hand as they stood. "My son—and my daughter—love you very much."

"I love them very much, too."

"I can see that. I . . . I just hope that the only tears they ever cry over you in the future will be tears of joy."

"I can't promise that. But I'm gonna do everything to make sure they are."

She squeezed his hand. "And *I'll* do everything to make sure you *do*."

"Don't be a stranger," Ann said as she hugged Raheim.

"He won't be," Ruth answered for him as she headed down the stoop.

"Drive safely," Mitchell advised, standing in the doorway.

"Shall do," Ann promised.

Destiny, standing next to her father, waved. "Good-bye, Gran'ma. Good-bye, Aunt Ruth."

"Bye Sweetie Pie."

"Bye Sugar Dumplin'."

Ann opened their car doors. "And thanks again for a great meal, darlin'. Anderson's gonna love these leftovers."

"So will Free. And so will I," added Ruth.

Mitchell, Raheim, and Destiny watched as the two women climbed into Ann's green Camry. Ann honked her horn as she drove off.

Raheim sighed. "Well . . . I guess I should be goin', too."

"No, you can't go now," Destiny protested, taking his hand. "Errol didn't get home yet."

"Uncle Raheim saw him last night," Mitchell reminded her.

"But I want him to have fun with us."

Mitchell looked at Raheim; the ball was in his court.

"Well . . . I guess I can stay until he gets back."

"*Yay!*" Destiny screamed, pulling him into the house.

Raheim shrugged; Mitchell chuckled.

Destiny wanted Raheim and her father to watch her favorite scenes from *The Wiz*, so they did. Destiny sat between them on the sofa in the family room. As Destiny sang to "He's the Wizard," "Soon as I Get Home," "I'm a Mean Ole Lion," "Don't Nobody Bring Me No Bad News," "If You Believe," and "Home," her father hummed and her uncle grooved along. Mitchell and Raheim caught each other stealing glances a half-dozen times. They'd always look away, busted yet blushing.

Destiny was showing Raheim the new words she learned from *My First Webster's Dictionary*—Mitchell'd purchased it for Errol when he was Destiny's age; Errol passed it on to Destiny last year—as they sat at the dining-room table, when she heard a key unlock the first-floor door.

"*Errol's home!*" Destiny raced to meet him. "*Hi, Errol!*"

He hunched down to hug her. "Hay, Little Bitty Pretty One." He tweaked her nose, the way her father used to do his.

She giggled. "I have a surprise for you."

"You do?"

"Uh-huh." She pulled him.

Errol was pleasantly surprised to see his father. "Dad."

"Hay, son."

"What are you doing here?"

"Visiting," Destiny responded for him.

"I see."

"He was waiting for you to get home."

"And you been keeping him company, huh?"

"Uh-huh. Me and Daddy."

"Ah."

Her daddy came downstairs. "Hey. How was your day?"

"It was jood."

"Did you eat dinner?"

"Yeah. But I can eat again."

"Of course."

"Believe me, you'll want to," his father assured him.

"Can I eat, too, Daddy?" Destiny pleaded.

"No. It's seven-thirty and you know what that means: time to take your bath and get ready for bed."

"Aw, Daddy," she groaned.

"Aw, Daddy, what?"

"I wanna stay up."

"Well, you can't."

She folded her arms across her chest. "I can, too."

Mitchell drew back. "Excuse me, young lady?"

"I can, too," she repeated, very defiant.

Raheim jumped in. "Now, Destiny: you know you not supposed to talk to your daddy like that, right?"

She stared at the floor.

He lifted her head by her chin. "Right?"

"Right," she whispered.

"And, you also know that if you don't take your bath and get ready for bed, Uncle Raheim won't tell you a bedtime story, right?"

Her eyes bugged. "You're gonna tell me a bedtime story?"

"Only if you take your bath and get ready for bed."

"*Oooh...*" she squealed.

"*And*, you tell your daddy you're sorry."

She wasn't too thrilled about that part. She slowly walked over to her father. "I'm sorry, Daddy."

He knelt down. "I accept your apology." They hugged.

She smiled at Raheim. "I'll be waiting for you."

"Okay. I'll be there."

She proceeded to tear up the stairs.

"Stop!" Mitchell demanded.

She did. She turned at the bottom step. "Sorry." She giggled. She walked up.

Mitchell giggled himself. "I'm going to help her. I'll be back down in a bit."

Errol put down his bag and sat in the antique chair by the entryway. "How long you been here?"

"Since four."

"Ah. You should've told me you were coming back today. I would've cut my time with the crew."

"How are Roe and Sid?"

"They're jood."

"What did y'all do today?"

"Nothin' much. A little studying. Played some slamball. And we watched *Apollo 13*."

"That musta been your pick."

"Yeah. Sort of a belated birthday screening."

"Did they enjoy it?"

"Well, Roe fell asleep a half hour into the movie. I'm surprised he lasted that long. And Sid hung in there, but I could tell he was just doin' it for me."

"They're really jood friends."

"Yeah. Uh, you wanna eat with me?"

"I'm kinda full, but I think I can have a little somethin'."

———————————

Errol handled the vegetables; Raheim cut their meat.

Raheim retrieved two glasses from the dishwasher. "What do you want to drink?"

"What are you having?"

"Water. I haven't had my daily recommended ten glasses."

"Me neither. I guess one is better than none."

After their plates were nuked in the microwave, they sat across from each other at the island. Errol said a silent prayer.

"You could've said it out loud, son."

"I know. But I think it's rude to assume everyone you break bread with will want to say grace."

"Like me?"

"Not necessarily you. I do it regardless of who I eat with or where I am. You . . . still don't believe in God?"

"Uh . . . I don't believe *in* God. And I don't believe in *a* God. But I do believe there is somethin' out there—or up there— that holds this world in balance. After goin' through the . . . puttin' myself through the fire and bein' brought out, there's got to be. There ain't no other explanation for it."

Errol nodded. "Um . . . are you still attending your meetings?"

"I went to my last one on Friday. Well, I believe it'll be my last one. It was also my hundredth."

"Wow, Dad. I read somewhere the average number of meetings people attend is twenty-one."

"Hmm. I guess I'm either a slow learner or got addicted to goin'."

"Nah. They went to twenty-one, but they probably *needed* twenty-two, or fifty-two, or a hundred and two."

"Yeah. Some of them probably thought twenty-one was still their lucky number."

"You did it until you felt you didn't need to anymore. And that's jood news. There's somethin' to toast."

They did.

"I've got more jood news."

"What?"

"I've been offered the lead in a movie."

"You have?"

"Yeah. I'm gonna tell them I accept it tomorrow."

"That's great, Dad! Congrats!"

"Thanks."

"What's the role?"

"Uh . . . I'll be playin' Glenn Burke."

"Glenn Burke?"

"Yeah."

Errol considered it. "Mmm . . ."

"How do you feel about that?"

"What do you mean?"

"Does it . . . bother you?"

"Why would it bother me?"

"Well, he was gay."

Errol shrugged. "O-kay . . ."

"That doesn't bother you?"

"No. Why would it?"

"Well, it seemed like you were . . . surprised when I said who it was."

"I was. But not because of who he was."

"No? Then why?"

"Because of who you are."

Raheim's eyebrows raised. "Me?"

"Yeah. I guess I never thought you would play that kind of role."

He knows me very well.

"But what if your friends put me down and put you down because of it. How would you feel?"

Errol shrugged. "Then they aren't really my friends."

That's my son.

"Besides," Errol added, "if your *being* gay doesn't bother me, why should your *playing* gay?"

There was that music, uh laughter, again.

"When will you start filming?"

"Probably as soon as possible. The movie's been in development for six years."

"So I guess we won't be having our monthly dinner . . . ?"

It's a ritual Raheim instituted three years ago, similar to the "getting to know you" dates Raheim had with his own father after he reappeared, so that he never loses touch with his son again. "Oh, yes, we will. If it means they gotta fly you in, it's gonna happen."

"Jood. That means I won't miss my allowance, either."

They giggled.

"I guess you won't be around to visit the schools with me," Errol said, looking down at his plate.

"If I gotta take a red-eye to meet you and then hop back on a plane that night, that's what I'm gonna do. Ain't no way I'm gonna let my Li'l Brotha—" Raheim caught himself. Now it was his turn to stare at his food.

Errol grinned. He might not look or feel like a Li'l Brotha Man anymore but he knows that's who he will forever be in his father's eyes. Hearing just a part of the title made him tingle. "I know how important this role is for your career. If you can't make it, I'll understand," Errol offered.

His father didn't accept that. "No you won't. And *I* won't, either. You've had to understand way too much, way too young, for way too long." Mitchell, Raheim's parents, Crystal, even Angel—they'd all had to make excuses for Raheim at one time or another. Raheim was determined to make sure those days were over. "Get anything new from the top four?"

"Yesterday, from Yale. The president of the Black Students Alliance wants to take me to dinner when I visit."

"Cool. But you sure you wanna go to Dubya's alma mater?"

Errol chuckled. "I won't hold him against them. Besides, they have a jood astronomy program. And, they *are* offering that scholarship."

"Well, don't go because the tuition may be free."

"I don't wanna break your bank."

"You let *me* worry about the finances, a'ight? They keep comin' correct, though: they know if anybody can bring back up their curve, you can." Raheim noticed Errol flinched when he said that. "Uh . . . you feelin' any pressure?"

"Pressure?"

"Yeah. You *are* the first Rivers man to go to college. And you'll be going at an age when, unlike many of your peers, you can't even vote."

Errol shrugged. "I don't know. Maybe a little."

"The last thing we want is for things to overwhelm you, to stress you out. You got a lot of important decisions to make, a lot to deal with. So, if it gets to be more than you can handle, you let us know." He didn't want to speak it, but Raheim was worried about him becoming an addict like his father and grandfather.

Raheim didn't say it, but Errol had a jood idea who made up that "we" and "us." "I will."

"And . . . are you scared?" Mitchell had mentioned to Raheim that he might be.

"Kinda," Errol mumbled.

"It's okay to be scared, son. Like the show says, it's gonna be a different world from where you come from. And, if anybody knows that it ain't gonna be easy bein' away from home . . ." Raheim sighed. "But that's more than a year away. You're gonna be a senior, and that kinda membership *does* have its privileges. The senior trip. The prom. Bein' the envy of all the underclassmen and gettin' the eye from all the underclass women . . . those are the things you should be concerned with. So make sure you enjoy it."

Errol's eyebrows raised. "There *is* a particular ring that would help me celebrate my senior year in style ..."

"So long as it don't cost as much as the teeth in O.D.B.'s mouth, you got it."

There goes their song again. They concentrated on their plates.

"Son?"

"Yes?"

"Uh ... I don't know how to ask this."

"Just ask. I don't have to be afraid to tell you something, and you don't have to be afraid to tell me something. Remember?"

Yeah, I remember ...

"Uh ... are you still angry with me?"

"Angry with you? About what?"

"You know, over how things went down. Me ... gettin' sick. Disappearin' on you 'n' Lit—Mitchell."

Errol grinned at that slipup. He pondered this query carefully. "I don't know if I was all that angry. I was more disappointed."

"I've ... disappointed you a lot."

"You're not perfect. No one is."

"I know I said it before, but I'm sorry."

"I know. I forgive you. I forgave you some time ago."

"You did?"

"Yeah. I saw that if you could forgive Grandpa, I could forgive you." Errol leaned in closer. "And Uncle Mitch has, too."

He's so sharp it scares me.

"You wanna play *Jeopardy!* after you read to Destiny?" Errol asked.

"Sure. I haven't played in ... years."

"I'll try to have mercy on you."

"Oh, you will?"

"Of course. I wouldn't want a man of your years to have to strain his brain too much." Errol chuckled.

"You only fifteen; you don't even know all the ways to *use* your brain yet."

"And you can teach me how?" It wasn't a challenge; it was an expectation.

Raheim smiled. "I sure can."

Mitchell peeked into Destiny's room. She was in her pink long-sleeve Strawberry Shortcake pajama suit, sitting up with her legs crossed, her elbows on her thighs and her fists under her chin, looking and listening intensely as Raheim, seated on the hall ottoman, finished Little Bill's *Elephant on the Loose*.

Raheim closed the book. "Did you enjoy that?"

"Uh-huh. Thank you." She hugged him.

"You're welcome. You repeated it, word for word. You must have heard it lots of times."

"Uh-huh. It's my favorite. Sometimes Daddy reads it and sometimes Errol does. But I like the way you read it best."

"Thanks." He turned to place the book back.

"No, read it again, *pleeze*?"

"Baby Doll, you gotta go to sleep."

"But I got a little more time left. See . . . ." She pointed to her elephant clock. "The little hand is on the eight and the big hand is on the five. I have five more minutes until lights-out!"

"You don't want your song?" Mitchell interjected. She gets one every Sunday night.

"Um . . . may I have both?"

"There's not enough time for both. But I could *sing* you a story if you want."

Destiny recognized the facial expression and the tone in her father's voice. "Oooh. You mean 'Fly'?"

"Yes."

"*Joody!* Uncle Raheim, you have to stay and hear it, too."

"Okay."

Destiny hopped off the bed. She got on her knees and clasped her hands. "Now I lay me down to sleep, I pray the Lord my soul to keep. If I should die before I wake, I pray the Lord my soul to take. God bless Daddy, and Gran'ma, and Gran'pa, and Errol, and Aunt Ruth . . . and Uncle Raheim. Amen."

Destiny scooted back in bed and folded her arms over the covers. Mitchell sat on the left side of her bed, placing his hands on top of hers. He began singing about the unorthodox friendship between a spider that hasn't "spun a single silver thread since 1968" and a fly that, as a poet, steals his inspiration from the Sunday *New York Times*.

"I just wanna give you a sweet . . ." Mitchell crooned. He kissed her on her forehead. ". . . sweet . . ." Then her nose. ". . . sweet . . ." Then her mouth. "Jood night, Sugar Plum."

"Jood night, Daddy," she whispered.

Raheim leaned in and kissed her on the right cheek. "Jood night, Baby Doll."

"Jood ni . . ." was all she could muster.

Raheim turned out her light. Mitchell smiled at her as he closed her door.

"That was beautiful," Raheim complimented.

"Thanks."

"It's obvious where Destiny gets her voice from."

Mitchell gushed.

"I never heard that song before. Who recorded it?"

"Lena Horne. She did it in her one-woman show on Broadway."

"Ah. It's the perfect lullaby."

"Mmm-hmm. That's why she says her prayers before. By the time the song is over, she's off to dreamland."

They stood in silence, studying their shoes.

Dressed in his nightclothes (a gray baseball tee and black cotton leisure pants), Errol emerged from his room with the

Jeopardy! box under his left arm. "I'm ready when you are, Dad."

Errol took the first game, his father the second.

"You came back strong," Errol noted.

"I came *back* strong? You make it sound like I was way behind. You only answered one more question right and won."

"True. For an old man, you can keep up."

They smiled.

Errol began setting up for another game. "We gotta have a tiebreaker."

"We do, but it's after eleven. You should be asleep."

"I can function on less than seven hours."

"You probably can, but that wouldn't be best."

"Come on, Dad. I'm fifteen, not five."

"I don't want you draggin' yourself from class to class. We got a GPA to keep."

Errol frowned, putting the pieces to the game inside the box.

It had been years since Raheim had seen him pout. And for him to do it at this age . . . it made Raheim smile inside. "We can pick up our battle another time."

"When?" Errol perked up.

"How about next Sunday?"

"You sure you wanna spend Father's Day gettin' trounced?"

They laughed. *Uh-huh, music.*

Raheim shrugged. "That's a chance I don't mind takin'."

"Okay. Thanks for helping me prepare."

"Prepare?"

"Yeah, for the *Jeopardy!* Teen Tournament. I'll be trying out when they come to town next month."

"Ah. I always wanted to go on the show."

"You still can. It's not too late."

He nodded. "No. It's not."

"We can be the first father-and-son champs."

"Hmm. Now that would be somethin'."

"Oh, I gotta take out the trash. Excuse me."

Raheim watched as he also made sure the back door was locked and the alarm was on (things Raheim used to do). Raheim met him at the bottom of the stairs. "This was fun, son."

"Yeah. You need to come around . . . more."

"I will." He hugged him. "You have a jood night."

"Ain't you gonna tuck me in, like Destiny?"

There was their song again.

"You're a little big for that. But I'll make sure you tuck *yourself* in jood."

Errol grinned. Raheim followed him upstairs.

"Jood night, Unc." Errol waved as they passed the great room.

Mitchell was sitting on the sofa—his back against the left armrest, his knees bent—reading the script. "Jood night."

As Raheim stood just outside his door, Errol turned on his iTunes visual (Lizz Wright's "Open Your Eyes, You Can Fly" began to play), climbed under the covers, and clasped his hands behind his head.

"Jood night, son."

"Jood night, Dad."

"I love you." Raheim hadn't said it to him in a while.

"And I love you, too, times two!"

Like the Supremes, Raheim heard a symphony as he shut off Errol's light and closed his door.

As Mitchell closed the script, Raheim sat next to him.

"So, whatcha think?"

Mitchell placed it on the coffee table. He smiled. He pre-

tended to open an envelope. "And the Oscar goes to . . . Raheim
Errol Rivers Jr."

"Ya think so?"

"Definitely. If Denzel can win as a corrupt cop, you can win
as a closeted baseball player."

"I ain't Denzel."

"No, you're not. But he won playing the Bad Negro and Sidney, the Good Negro. This role doesn't fall on either side of
those extremes; it's in the middle. Glenn is presented as a de-
cent, flawed man with an age-old dilemma—to be or not to
be—and we get to see how he decides to be. So our third time
will definitely be the charm. You'll be breaking new ground.
How many Black actors play a gay role in which they don't drag
up or queen out?"

"True."

"I'm sure many turned it down because it isn't camp; they
can't coon their way through it. So the fact that he's gay but
acts, looks, and talks like a so-called straight man will also work
in your favor. The majority of female voters will be attracted to
him and the majority of male voters will view him as just one
of the guys. And it won't hurt that you've battled an addiction.
They love to reward folks who have overcome obstacles, been
through the fire. Some will view this as your comeback."

"My *comeback*? With a comeback, you comin' back to the
spot you left. I'm in a different place now. It's . . . it's more like
a rebirth."

"When they throw comeback in your face, that should be
your comeback."

They chuckled.

"There are a lot of juicy moments. But, as with Diane Lane
in *Unfaithful*, everyone will be talking about that one scene."

"You mean, the part where I, uh, he has sex for the first time
and realizes what it really means?"

"Yup. You will have gone through every emotion in that one moment that many of us have and still do. I can just hear Ebert and Roeper raving about it now. I see you've already claimed the role as your own."

Raheim nodded.

"Some folks won't be ready for it; there's still fallout over the rumors about Mike Piazza and the player supposedly involved with that editor at *OUT*. And I didn't know Glenn introduced the high-five to baseball thirty years ago—that'll make many straight jocks in and outside of the pro-sports world squirm." Mitchell leaned forward. "The role will require a lot of you. You'll probably have to go through some sort of spring training." He knuckled Raheim in the chest with his middle finger. "But you're rather well preserved for a thirty-one-year-old, so that shouldn't be a problem."

Raheim giggled.

"I'm sure your son will be glad to give you a few pointers on the game. And, if you won't be, I bet he'd love to play Glenn as a teenager."

"Ha, he already put his bid in for that."

"And, you've gotta *sing*, in a *church choir*. I can't wait to hear that!"

"Uh, will you help me out with that?"

"Of course." Mitchell studied him. "Some of the scenes . . . they may be . . . emotionally intense."

"I can handle it. I guess everything I've been through . . . it's kinda prepared me for it. I . . . I can identify with him in a lot of ways."

"How?" Mitchell knew how; he just wanted to hear it.

"Not bein' able to . . . be yourself. Afraid of what people are gonna think, say." Raheim peered at him. "Hidin' the one I love from the others I love."

"Mmm. Something he says reminds me of you, too."

"What?"

" 'I didn't think you could be gay and not be a sissy.' "

Raheim waved that comment off. "I don't think like that no more."

Mitchell was glad to hear that—and knew he meant it. "And . . . I'm sure you'll be asked *the* question."

"Yeah."

"What will you say?"

Raheim considered it. "Somethin' like, 'I'm not gay, but my man is.' "

They howled.

"*Jood* answer," Mitchell affirmed. "Nathan Lane couldn't have said it better. Gene will be shocked. Babyface will be proud. And B.D.? He'll want to throw you a coming-*way*-out party."

"I bet he will."

"And he won't be the only one. If the white queens lusted you before as a model, they're gonna love you because of this role. But some of the Children won't be celebrating, since you're surrounded by whites in the film."

"You gonna be in that group . . . ?" Raheim mumbled.

"Of course not. Now, would I prefer this was, say, an adaptation of an E. Lynn Harris novel, where you'd have a better chance of being in the arms of another brother? Yes. But, apparently, that wasn't Glenn's life. Speakin' of: How do you feel about the love scenes?" Mitchell already knew that, too.

"I'm not feelin' kissin' a white boy," Raheim groused.

"*A* white boy? I counted three. And, you do more than kiss one of them."

"Don't remind me."

"That one scene is a little explicit, but it's important to the story. It may end up on the cutting-room floor though. Because the players walk around naked and talk trash about women in the locker room, it's guaranteed an R. That scene will definitely bump it up to an NC-17."

"And don't forget about the naked groupies."

"Mmm-hmm . . . this'll probably be the first time male groupies in professional sports will be portrayed. Uh . . . have you ever found a naked man in *your* hotel room like Glenn?"

Hmm . . . he never asked that question while we were together. Guess he feels safe asking it now . . . "Nah. But there's been plenty that wanted to get naked *in* my hotel room."

"I'm sure."

Raheim huffed. "I just don't wanna be kissin' a troll."

Mitchell laughed. "If it'll help, you can pretend you're kissing me."

He placed his hand on Mitchell's. "I'd rather not pretend."

They hadn't touched in any way in years. Mitchell drew in a quick breath; as he silently let it out, he folded his hand onto Raheim's. They smiled.

"Are you ready to be annointed *the* spokesperson for the Black gay/lesbian/bi/SGL/queer/transgendered/transsexual/two-spirit community?" Mitchell asked sarcastically.

Raheim chuckled. "What's that?"

"I know, right? But you'll be the most visible member of the tribe, so you'll be expected to speak for all of us. I know at least one person who will be giving you the third-degree."

"Who?"

"Roe."

"For real?"

"Yup. Ever since Errol told him his godfather is gay, he's had twenty *million* questions. Finding out about me shocked his world; finding out about you is gonna *rock* his world."

"Mmm . . . I thought E. woulda told him by now. And Sid."

"I think Errol's waiting for the right time to tell them."

"Ha, *somebody* told me a long time ago there ain't no such thing as *the right time*."

Mitchell acknowledged that with a nod. "He's waiting for the right *person* to do it. One thing's for certain: Roe's father won't be pleased to know that his best friend's father not only plays a homo in a movie but *is* one."

"Then I guess we gonna hafta work on him, too."

"And are you ready for *every* detail of your private life to be fodder for the tabloids?" Mitchell joked.

"I was just on international TV talkin' about my gamblin' problem. I ain't got nothin' to hide."

"You don't think so? I got a few tales *I* could sell to the *National Inquirer*."

"Sell away—so long as *I* get a cut."

They laughed.

"As I've learned, you can work the bad publicity—it all comes down to spin. Uh . . . you gonna come with me to the Oscars?"

"Ooh, the chance to rub elbows with Halle and kee-kee with Jada? If you're still single, it's a date."

"If you're my date, I won't be."

They grinned.

Raheim settled back but leaned in to the left, moving a little closer to him. "So, tell me about the job."

Mitchell took the fax off the coffee table and handed it to him. After Raheim read it over, Mitchell filled him in on the conversation he'd had with Em. By the time he was done, Raheim's arms were draped across Mitchell's legs, which were stretched across Raheim's thighs.

"They would want to be comin' at you like that. You deserve it."

"Thanks."

"Sounds like a great opp."

"It is."

"But . . . ?" Raheim knew Mitchell had reservations—or, rather, one. And he knew what that reservation was. . . .

"I . . . I just don't know if now is the right time."

Raheim's eyebrows rose. "*Right* time?"

Mitchell breathed a chuckle. "The *best* time to do something like this."

"Why wouldn't it be?"

"I do have a full house."

Raheim stated the obvious. "E. is goin' away to college next year. And Destiny ain't a baby no more. In fact, things are fallin' into place the way we . . . you planned."

"What do you mean?"

"You know. That you would stay home with Destiny until she went to the first grade."

He remembered. "Yeah. Boy, those years flew by."

"Uh-huh. They grow up . . . and away. And Destiny's really independent. It's time she really saw that her daddy can be, too."

Mitchell was thrown by that comment. "Huh?"

"Well, you been there for her ever since she was born—right there."

Mitchell became a little defensive. "I was *supposed* to be."

"Of course you was supposed to be. You've given her a life many kids don't get. But, like I said, she ain't a baby. You can't be afraid to let go."

"Let go?"

"Yeah. You armed her with the tools to go out in the world and make a space for herself and she's already doing that in her own way. Now you gotta give yourself permission to do what you want for you, knowin' that what you do will make things better for the both of y'all. That's gonna be another jood lesson for her: she'll know where that independence can take her."

Mitchell looked at Raheim quizzically. "You been watchin' *Dr. Phil?*"

They laughed.

"Actually, yeah. The past few days. I'm goin' on his show next month."

Mitchell knew what the topic would be. "You're becoming, what they call on the talk show circuit, an 'expert.' "

"Not an expert, just experienced. That's how I know it ain't gonna be easy, lettin' go. I'm still tryin' to do it with Li'l . . . E."

"So I hear."

"We can't keep 'em little forever. We gotta cut the cord. She can survive. And you can too."

Silence.

"It's . . . gonna be scary," Mitchell admitted.

"What is?"

"Being . . . out there. I haven't been out there in so long."

"You make it sound like another planet."

"In a way it will be. I haven't punched a time clock as a journalist in ten years. The world is a much different place."

"It is. But you'll be coming at it differently, as the E-I-C. And you can handle it. The question is can *it* handle *you.* It may not be able to take you and Emil."

"Hmm . . . two Black SGL men helming Black magazines not specifically for Black SGL people. That would be major. Funny, but I never thought of that."

"I bet they have. They probably don't want you wavin' a rainbow flag . . ."

"You know I won't be."

"Yeah. But they gotta know your bein' SGL is gonna draw attention to the magazine."

"And it's all about spin."

"Right."

"Hmmph. No wonder the letter mentions race *and* sexual orientation as issues the company takes seriously. Because of that, I should ask for twice the money."

They laughed.

Mitchell sighed. "That means I may have to have *that* talk with Destiny."

"You haven't already?"

"No. We've talked about there being different kinds of families in the world. But not that her daddy is a Same-Gender-Loving man."

"How did that topic come up?"

"At the beginning of the school year, she made a friend named Tammy, who has a mother and a stepmother. She wanted to know how this could be."

"What did you tell her?"

"That some children only have a daddy, like she does. Some only have a mommy. Some have both a mommy and daddy, some have two daddies like Errol, and some have two mommies like Tammy. Sometimes the parents that made you don't raise you—and that's not a bad thing. Look at Tammy: she lives with her stepmother. And look at us."

"Mmm. I remember when I told Li'l...E. about us. I couldn't even say the *word gay*..."

Li'l Brotha Man, you know what it means when two people are together, right?

Uh-huh. That means they a couple.

Right. And who can make up a couple?

A man and a woman.

Right. But, a man and a woman... they not the only two people that can make a couple.

What do you mean, Daddy?

A man can be with a woman. But a man can also be with a man. And a woman with a woman. They all couples. Just different kinds.

How can that be, Daddy? A man and a woman get married and have a baby. Like you and Mommy. But you didn't get married.

That's right. But the way a person feels for someone else...it don't have to have anything to do with havin' a baby or gettin' married. See... there are some men who just have feelings for women. And there are some men who just have feelings for men. And then there are some men who have feelings for men and women. Like me.

You have feelings for men and women?

Yeah.

Like...I have feelings for you, and I have feelings for Mommy?

No, Li'l Brotha Man. It's different. The way you feel for me and Mommy, that's how a parent and child feel about each other. What I'm talkin' about...I had feelings for your mom and now I have the same kind of feelings for...Mitchell.

Mitch-hull?

Yeah.

How can you do that?

It's...it's just natural for me. I feel really close to Mitchell the way I used to feel close to Mommy. But that don't mean I don't have feelings for Mommy. I still care for her. But...I feel closer to Mitchell now.

Oh. Do Mommy know you and Mitchell...close?

Yeah, she do. And, to be honest with you, she's not too happy about it.

Why?

'Cause...now she likes Mitchell a lot, and she loves the way he's been a godfather to you. You like that, too, right?

Uh-huh, I do.

She knows you mean a lot to him. But...she's a little uncomfortable with our bein' together. You know what that word mean, uncomfortable?

Uh-huh. That's when something bothers you.

Right. It's not that she don't like Mitchell. It's that me and Mitchell bein' a couple, loving each other...I guess its hard for her to accept.

So...you love Mitch-hull?

Yeah, I do.

And… Mitch-hull loves you?

Yeah. Some people think that it's wrong for people like me and Mitchell to be together.

What kind of people are you, Daddy?

Two men… who love each other. But when two people love each other, that's a jood thing.

I love you. And I love Mitch-hull. Will people think that's wrong?

Some people might. But you know in your heart that it ain't wrong.

Um, how long you and Mitch-hull been a couple, Daddy?

Uh… like four years.

Wow. That's a long time. It's like you married.

Uh, kinda sorta, yeah. We not married but we love you like a married couple would.

That means we a family.

Right. Me, you, and Lit—Little Bit, we a family.

Who is Little Bit, Daddy?

That's what I call Mitchell. Like, your nickname is Li'l Brotha Man, his nickname is Little Bit.

Oh. Why do you call him that?

'Cause, standin' next to your daddy, he's a little bit of a man. He shorter and weighs less than me. But he's got a big heart.

That's what Grammy said about Mitch-hull, too.

Grammy is right.

Daddy?

Yeah?

Why didn't you tell me before?

Well, Li'l Brotha Man… when me and Little Bit became a couple, you was so young… I… I didn't know what to say… or how to say it… so that you would understand.

You coulda told me back then, Daddy.

I could?

Uh-huh. I liked Mitch-hull from the first time I met him. Like I liked Winston the first time I met him. When Mommy got married to Winston, he became my stepfather; what do I call Mitch-hull?

I don't know, man. You can talk to him and choose somethin' together.

Okay.

So, are you comfortable with me and Little Bit bein' a couple?

I think so.

Jood. You lucky, Li'l Brotha Man. Your mommy and daddy both got somebody in their lives that love them and love you. And that means you get twice the love from us.

Ooh...like to the second power?

Yup. Like to the second power.

That's a jood thing. If it's twice as much that means it's twice as jood!

Ya know it.

"... so, tryin' to break that concept down is gonna be an even bigger challenge. But, like you said: 'They may not be able to put it into words, but they know.' "

"Mmm-hmm. She acts the same way around us Errol did at her age."

Silence.

"Have you thought of a name for the magazine?"

"I was thinking of...*Rise*."

"Hmm. Why *Rise*?"

"It's a nod to Maya's poem. What I hope we can do is help readers understand that, no matter what they have or may be going through or will face, they can rise above and beyond it."

"You sound like Iyanla."

They chuckled.

"Maybe she can do a column. Or Maya. And I'd like to publish monthly essays from celebrities talking about a pivotal moment in their lives as children that shaped who they are."

"Mmm...maybe I can do one."

"Indeed. And we'll be putting you on the cover."

"Won't that be a conflict of interest?"

"How?"

"Putting your . . . ex on the cover." He'd never referred to himself as that to Mitchell before. He hoped he'd never have to again.

"You will be playing a man many of us don't know about and should. It's not our fault we were . . . once a couple." Mitchell had never referred to their union in the past tense to Raheim before—and he, too, hoped it would be the last time.

"Ha, is that what you gonna tell your peers?"

"Yes. Think they'll buy it?"

"No."

"Like I care? We're living in the era of the *un*fair and *un*balanced Fox News. If anything, the controversy will help sell magazines. And movie tickets. All about spin."

"See, you're beginning to think like the E-I-C."

They breathed together. Just like they used to.

Mitchell rose. "I'll be right back."

He returned with a tray and sat it down on the coffee table. He handed Raheim the champagne bottle. "Will you do the honors?"

When the cork popped, Mitchell caught much of the bubbly splashing out with one of the glasses. Raheim finished filling them.

"Here's to . . . new beginnings," Mitchell toasted.

"I'll drink to that. And . . . uh . . . happy anniversary."

Wow, Mitchell thought. *We met exactly ten years ago this evening.* Raheim was always jood about remembering things like that; he wasn't. But after they split, he found himself remembering . . . and wishing. The smile on his face told Raheim he, too, had remembered—and it was something he wanted to remember.

They clinked. They sipped. They sat back, shoulder to shoulder, each slightly leaning on the other.

"What are your plans for Father's Day?" Raheim inquired.

"I'm going to the Wall. I'll be taking Destiny. She's asked about my father. I told her he died fighting a war. She wanted me to point out Vietnam on her globe. She said it looked like he was a million miles away from home."

"How y'all goin' to D.C.?"

"Amtrak. She loves taking the train. She's been to Richmond to see her grandfather's relatives a couple of times."

"Uh, if you want . . . I can drive down."

Mitchell was touched by the offer. "I . . . we'd love that, very much. But, don't you want to spend the day with *your* father?"

"I think he'd understand. Besides, every day is Father's Day for him."

"And what about your son? He may have plans for you two."

"He does. He wants to break our tie and be crowned the *Jeopardy!* champ."

"Ah. I played him a few times and, as with his father, could never beat him."

"He'll probably wanna go with us. I think he'd appreciate the Wall."

"Yeah. He would."

The radio was on, but they weren't paying much attention to it. But they did when . . .

"Welcome back to *Midnight After Dark*. I'm your host, Mr. Magic, and here's Luther's new one, 'Dance with My Father.' The CD of the same name hits stores next week . . ."

Mitchell grabbed the remote and turned up the volume. "Oh. Have you heard it yet?"

"No."

"Me neither."

After the first verse and chorus, Mitchell began to cry. But Raheim saw it comin'—he had Mitchell's glass out of his hands and back on the tray, and had Mitchell wrapped up in his right arm before the first tear fell. He held him as he continued to cry after the song went off.

Mitchell lifted his head, which had been buried in Raheim's chest. "Thanks."

Raheim thumbed away the tracks of his tears. "You don't have to thank me. *I'm* the one that should be thankin' *you*."

"Thanking me? Why?"

"For lovin' E. like he's your own. For bein' there for me when I didn't deserve it. For just bein' you."

Mitchell sniffled. He looked down. "I've gotten your father's shirt all wet."

"It'll dry."

As René Moore began the first verse to "You Don't Have to Cry," Mitchell returned his head to *his* spot on Raheim's chest and Raheim's arm, which had dropped to Mitchell's waist when he sat up, clutched him tighter *there* and pulled him in closer.

They breathed together as the songs told their story: Chaka Khan's "Love Me Still"; Patti LaBelle's "Love and Learn"; Miles Jaye's "Next Time"; Chante Moore & Kenny Lattimore's "Still"; Wendy Moten's "Come In Out of the Rain"; Jeffrey Osbourne's "We're Going All The Way"; Aretha and the Four Tops' "If Ever a Love There Was"; and Luther's "A House Is Not a Home."

After Luther's final *"Still in love...wi-i-i-ith me-e-e... yea-ea-eaaaa-aaaah,"* Raheim broke their silence. "Uh... Mitchell?"

Mitchell said nothing. He just breathed.

"Little Bit?" Raheim whispered.

Mitchell only shifted, pushing and snuggling in closer. He'd gotten less than eight hours of sleep since Friday, and not only was he going to catch up, he was going to do it in the arms he longed for, dreamed of being in again. And Raheim had no intention of interrupting that sleep.

For him, it was like being home again, too.

monday,
june 9, 2003

When Mitchell opened his eyes, he didn't hear Errol walking down the hall. Or closing the bathroom door. Or flushing the toilet. Or running the faucet or the shower. Or walking past his door to venture upstairs.

Why is it so quiet?

He looked over at the clock on the nightstand (something he never does in the morning) . . .

Eight o'clock!

He jumped out of bed, sprinting out of his room and down the hall. He didn't notice that he was still in his clothes from the day before—and that the only way he could've gotten upstairs is if Raheim had carried him.

He stopped at Destiny's bedroom door; it was open and her bed was made.

Even more surprising: Errol's bedroom door was open—and *his* bed was made!

Mitchell raced downstairs and followed the laughter coming from the breakfast nook. He stood in the foyer outside the kitchen.

"Jood morning, Daddy!" Destiny was seated at the breakfast table with Errol on her right and Raheim on her left.

"Well, jood morning." He approached them. "How come you all didn't wake me?"

Raheim rose. "I figured you could use the extra hours."

"Uncle Raheim cooked us breakfast."

"He did?" Mitchell knew it had to be a joke; Raheim had never cooked breakfast for him, and the one time he tried to make dinner it was a disaster.

"Yeah. I saved a plate for you." Raheim took it out of the top oven. He removed a tinfoil cover. He placed it on the table.

Mitchell looked at the dish. He looked at Raheim. "*You* cooked this?"

Raheim chuckled. "Yeah, *I* cooked this."

Mitchell eyed him suspiciously. "You sure this wasn't delivered courtesy of the twenty-four-hour diner on Flatbush Avenue?"

"They can't make home fries like these," promised Errol, wolfing his down.

Mitchell said a silent prayer over his food. The home fries *were* fabulous.

"Isn't it jood, Daddy?"

"Yes. Yes, it is." Mitchell's eyes flickered over to Raheim. "Where did you learn to cook?"

"My pops."

"Mmm..."

Errol popped up, taking his and Destiny's dishes over to the sink, rinsing them off, and placing them in the dishwasher.

Enjoying the breakfast, Mitchell realized they were about to leave. "Your lunch!"

Destiny stood up. "Uncle Raheim already made it." She took her lunch box from Raheim.

"He did?"

"Uh-huh. I got a peanut-butter-and-jelly sandwich, Oreo cookies, a apple, and raisins."

"Ah. I'm sure you can't wait for lunchtime to come."

Raheim knelt down on his left knee in front of her. "Bye, Baby Doll."

"Bye."

"I love you."

"I love you, too, times two!"

They hugged.

"Are you gonna be here when I get home from school?"

"Uh, I don't know."

She frowned.

"But if I can't be, I'll call you, okay?"

Her face lit up. "Okay. Make sure you call before *Dora the Explorer* is on."

"What time does she come on?"

"Three-thirty."

"I'll call you at three-twenty."

"Jood!"

Mitchell got up, wiping his mouth with a napkin. "Bye, Sugar Plum."

"Bye, Daddy."

He pinched her nose. "I love you."

She pinched his. "And I love you, too, times two!"

They embraced.

"Later, Dad." Errol raised his fist.

Raheim raised his and they "shook." "A'ight, son." He handed Errol his lunch (he has three PB&J sandwiches).

Errol turned to Mitchell. Mitchell once again aimed to pinch his nose—but for the first time in almost three years, Errol didn't flinch or move away. Instead of a pinch, Mitchell tapped it with his middle knuckle. Errol's smile said he approved of the new send-off.

Mitchell and Raheim followed them as they exited the front door. "You two have a jood day," they wished in unison. They glanced at each other. They blushed.

"We will," Destiny and Errol replied together, grinning back at them.

As she and Errol walked out the front gate, Destiny waved good-bye; her father and uncle waved back. She then took Errol's right hand and they made their way to the corner. Raheim and Mitchell stood in the doorway watching them. Mitchell leaned back, brushing Raheim's chest; Raheim leaned forward, gently settling against Mitchell. They exhaled as their children crossed the street and headed up the block.